12/22

Praise for Renée Watson

A *KIRKUS REVIEWS* BEST BOOK OF THE YEAR
A CHICAGO PUBLIC LIBRARY BEST BOOK OF THE YEAR

★ "Watson's heroine is smart and courageous,
bringing her optimistic attitude to any
challenge she faces."
—*Kirkus Reviews*, starred review

★ "Realistic snapshots of love in action are peppered
with funny mishaps and small mistakes, all of which
add up to an uplifting, reassuring read."
—*Booklist*, starred review

★ "Both relatable and inspirational. A young
optimistic Black girl, Watson's irresistible Ryan
models how to navigate a changing world
with resilience, kindness, and love."
—*School Library Journal*, starred review

"Ryan is an engaging heroine, with a creative streak
and a take-charge attitude." —*BCCB*

"An expert at creating complex characters, Watson
ensures that no one will be two dimensional.
This second installment about Ryan is every bit
as enjoyable as the first." —*Horn Book Magazine*

WAYS TO MAKE SUNSHINE

A *NEW YORK TIMES* BESTSELLER
AN INDIE BESTSELLER
A *NEW YORK TIMES* BEST CHILDREN'S BOOK OF THE YEAR
A *PARENTS* MAGAZINE BEST BOOK OF THE YEAR
A *SCHOOL LIBRARY JOURNAL* BEST BOOK OF THE YEAR
A *KIRKUS REVIEWS* BEST BOOK OF THE YEAR
A *PUBLISHERS WEEKLY* BEST BOOK OF THE YEAR
AN AMAZON BEST BOOK OF THE YEAR

"This brave new world we're living in sure could use more stories about these bright and imaginative girls who specialize in 'making a way out of no way.'" —*The New York Times Book Review*

★ "Intermittently funny, frustrating, and touching.... Allows Black readers to see themselves and all readers to find a character they can love. Move over, Ramona Quimby, Portland has another neighbor you have to meet!" —*Kirkus Reviews*, starred review

★ "Captures the uncertainty of growing up amid change through the eyes of an irrepressible Black girl." —*Publishers Weekly*, starred review

★ "Ryan Hart is a vivacious child . . . with personality and spirit reminiscent of some of the most well-loved heroines in classic juvenile fiction tales." —*Booklist*, starred review

★ "A fresh beginning to a new chapter book series featuring a girl who can coax out sunshine from behind the darkest storm." —*Shelf Awareness*, starred review

BY RENÉE WATSON

WAYS TO SHARE JOY

RENÉE WATSON

illustrated by Andrew Grey

BLOOMSBURY
CHILDREN'S BOOKS
NEW YORK   LONDON   OXFORD   NEW DELHI   SYDNEY

BLOOMSBURY CHILDREN'S BOOKS
Bloomsbury Publishing Inc., part of Bloomsbury Publishing Plc
1385 Broadway, New York, NY 10018

BLOOMSBURY, BLOOMSBURY CHILDREN'S BOOKS, and the Diana logo
are trademarks of Bloomsbury Publishing Plc

First published in the United States of America in September 2022 by
Bloomsbury Children's Books

Bloomsbury books may be purchased for business or promotional use. For
information on bulk purchases please contact Macmillan Corporate and Premium
Sales Department at specialmarkets@macmillan.com

Library of Congress Cataloging-in-Publication Data
Names: Watson, Renée, author.
Title: Ways to share joy / by Renée Watson.
Description: New York : Bloomsbury Children's Books, 2022.
Series: A Ryan Hart story; book 3
Summary: Ryan is caught between two friends who both want to be her
best friend, her brother ruins her latest baking project, and a classmate
keeps teasing her at school, yet Ryan still looks for a way to see the
bright side of things and not let anything steal her joy.
Identifiers: LCCN 2022017378 (print) | LCCN 2022017379 (e-book)
ISBN 978-1-5476-0909-3 (hardcover) ● ISBN 978-1-5476-0910-9 (e-book)
Subjects: CYAC: Family life—Fiction. | Best friends—Fiction. |
Friendship—Fiction. | African Americans—Fiction. | LCGFT: Novels.
Classification: LCC PZ7.1.S47 Wd 2022 (print) | LCC PZ7.1.S47 (e-book)
DDC [Fic]—dc23
LC record available at https://lccn.loc.gov/2022017378
LC e-book record available at https://lccn.loc.gov/2022017379

Book design by Yelena Safronova
Typeset by Westchester Publishing Services
Printed and bound in the U.S.A.
2 4 6 8 10 9 7 5 3 1

To find out more about our authors and books visit www.bloomsbury.com
and sign up for our newsletters.

*In loving memory of
Ms. Verna Fisher,
1945–2021*

CONTENTS

RYAN IN THE MIDDLE

I AM A GIRL IN the middle. Stuck in between my older brother, Ray, and baby sister, Rose. Being in the middle means I have my brother bossing me around telling me to do this, do that. It means I am called on to help out with baby Rose when she needs to be rocked, fed, changed. It means Ray gets more privileges because he is the oldest and can stay home by himself sometimes and gets to stay up later at night. Being in the middle means when we get in the back of the car, Rose is strapped in her car seat on the passenger's side—where I used to sit—and Ray is at the other window right behind the driver's seat.

I am in the middle.

So now it means it's harder to see the license plates of the other cars as they speed by, and Ray is getting a lot more points when we play our game, naming cars from out of town. It means that if Rose starts to cry while we're stuck in traffic, I am the one who takes her hand and tries to calm her. And when her pacifier slips out of her mouth, I am the one who puts it back in. Maybe this is why I am Rose's favorite.

She knows I will be there whenever she needs me because this is what big sisters do.

Some people only know how to be the oldest or the youngest, but I know all about being a little sister *and* a big sister. So this means, as we grow older, I'll be able to tell Ray not to pull Rose's hair because little sisters don't like getting their hair pulled. And I'll tell Rose that sometimes big brothers treat you like a delicate flower and think you can't race as fast, or that you can't keep up with the boys, and I'll tell her that we can and show her how. I'll teach her how to pull pranks and also how to come to us for help if she's ever afraid. And since I'm in the middle, and since I have to live up to my name, Ryan, and be a leader, I'll probably be the one to keep the peace whenever they argue.

Ryan in the middle, that's me.

Last night when I wrote in my memory journal, I tried to think of all the important things that are in the middle. Maybe I'll be like them. Sweet, like the best part of sandwich cookies—the filling. Strong like the bridges that are in the middle of two places, making it easy to get from here to there. Maybe I'll be like glue and keep us together.

But right now, I am not in the middle. I am sitting next to Ray on the sofa and Rose is in my arms. Mom is taking our pictures before Ray and I leave for the harvest festival at church. I am dressed up as a chef. Ray is the Black Panther. Rose isn't coming with us, but Mom still has her in a costume—a ladybug. They'll be home giving out candy to trick-or-treaters. Dad is at work, so Grandma is taking us to the party. Grandma made me an apron with my name stitched across the top in big curly letters. My chef hat sits on my head, hovering like a big cumulous cloud.

"Say *happy Halloween!*" Mom says.

I smile my biggest smile and the camera flashes.

"One more," Mom says. But she never just takes one more. She puts us in different poses and takes a lot more pictures. She even asks Grandma to get in some of them, even though Grandma does not have on a costume.

Just when I think it's about to become a photo shoot, Grandma says, "We've got to get going or we'll miss the whole event."

"All right. Last one," Mom says. She takes another photo and then she sets the phone down and reaches out for Rose. I hand my baby sister to my mom and kiss them both goodbye.

When we get to the church, we head down to the basement where the party is happening. There are decorations up, but nothing creepy or scary. I walk straight to the dessert contest station to submit my sugar cookies. "Well hello, Miss Ryan," Ms. Howard says. "How's that little sister of yours?"

"She's good," I tell her. I hand her my cookies.

"Well, how about that? Did you make these all by yourself?"

"Yes, ma'am," I say. "My dad helped me with the decorating, but I made the cookies and the frosting from scratch."

"I think you're the youngest contestant. Usually, the contest is full of us old folk," Ms. Howard says.

"Looks like Ms. Lee is going to have some fierce competition."

I smile. She sure is.

Ray and I walk over to where the teenagers are standing. The only reason I'm coming over here is because this is the station where the trick-or-treat bags are being handed out. It's also the station where Luke is. I just know he's going to tease me like he always does. He says hi to Ray and gives him a bag. Then he hands me my bag and says, "Here's Runaway Ryan."

"Stop calling me that," I tell him.

The Easter speech was a long, long time ago. I don't know why he's still bringing up that I couldn't finish my speech and ran off the stage. If he had been at church camp this past summer, he'd know I acted in my skit just fine, didn't mess up any of my lines.

Luke says, "Oh, I'm just messing with you. But if it hurts your feelings, I'll stop."

We both know he's not going to stop. Especially because right after he promises to stop, he points toward the other side of the fellowship hall and says, "Fast-Talking Bobby and Forgetful Gary are over there," calling them by the nicknames he gave them last Easter.

At least I'm not the only one.

Luke tells me and Ray, "They were looking for you earlier. KiKi, too."

We walk over to Bobby, Gary, and KiKi, who are at the Beanbag Toss station. KiKi is in line behind Bobby. "Hi, Ryan. I like your costume," KiKi says.

"I love yours!" I tell her. She is dressed up as Shuri. I know it's the only time her mom is going to let her wear makeup. She looks just like the Shuri poster hanging in her bedroom.

"What's up, Chef Ryan?" Bobby says.

"Hey." I want to ask him who he's dressed up as because I can't tell by the plain clothes he is wearing. But I don't ask because it's his turn to go up and try to toss the beanbags in the plastic pumpkin pails that are all spaced apart so that some are easy to make and others are hard.

Bobby goes for the harder ones first. He misses on his first try but gets the next three. It's KiKi's turn now. She has a different strategy, going for the easy ones and then the ones far away. Every time she makes one, she does a little dance. And since she's dressed up like Shuri, she is a dancing superhero. She throws the last beanbag and it hits the rim of the bucket but doesn't go in. "How did I miss that?" KiKi shouts.

"You'll still get a prize," Bobby says. "Everyone gets a prize." He sounds disappointed when he says this.

After Bobby and KiKi choose their prizes from the secret grab bag, we walk to the other stations. At our next stop, we play a guessing game trying to estimate how many candy corn are in the mason jar. Someone calls out one million, and of course that's impossible. I take a guess. "Two hundred fifty!" I call out.

And then Olivia makes a guess. "One hundred twenty-five!"

After all the guesses are made, Deacon LeRoy says, "There are two hundred seventy-five candy corn in this jar! That means, Ryan, you are the winner."

I hardly ever win anything, so even though it's just a chance to dig in the grab bag and pull out a random prize, it still feels like a big deal. Deacon LeRoy holds the big bag open as wide as it can go, and I reach in, moving things around that feel like thin paper— probably stickers, or bookmarks. I go for something bigger. My hand touches a round container. I pull it out. "Silly Putty! Yes!" KiKi shouts, as if the prize is hers. She knows I'm going to let her play with it, too, making slimy shapes together.

Everyone else who made a guess but didn't win gets to pick out of another bag—it's all candy in that bag. The trades start as soon as everyone has something. Chocolates for fruity candies, sours for sweets.

We walk over to the snack table to get something to drink. "I miss Amanda," I say to KiKi. "I wish she was here." Before Amanda moved, the three of us did everything together. She would have been here tonight, dressed up as an angel or something that requires sparkles. I expect for KiKi to say something about how she misses Amanda too, but she doesn't. She just keeps walking to the snack table and when we get there she picks up a cup of apple cider and starts drinking. "Did you hear me?" I ask. "I wish Amanda was here."

"I heard you," KiKi says. She takes another drink of apple cider. "But aren't we having fun? Just me and you?"

"Of course, yes. I just—I just miss it being the three of us sometimes."

"Is Amanda your best friend?" KiKi asks.

But I can't answer her because as soon as she asks the question, Ms. Howard calls out, "Okay, it's time to announce the winners of our dessert contest!"

My heart swells. This is the only competition I care about winning. And this is the only one where there really is a winner and not everyone who participates gets something. Each winner gets a gift basket of Moonstruck chocolates. There are only three ribbons being given out—first, second, third. The baskets of chocolates get bigger and fuller from third, to second, to first. I sure would love a basket of chocolate. Especially Moonstruck chocolate. I think about my chances—there were at least twenty desserts on that table. It's probably impossible that I'll beat out grown-ups who've been cooking and baking their whole lives.

We all crowd around the judging table. Ms. Howard calls off a few honorable mentions and then says, "For third place we have . . ." She pauses, making the announcement dramatic and keeping us in suspense. "Ms. Lee!"

People clap and Ms. Lee looks shocked. She always wins first place. Always she is the one getting the ribbon pinned on and always she is the one holding the too-big basket of Moonstruck chocolates, with bars that mix chocolate with orange, or caramel, or peanuts.

Ms. Lee walks up to receive her prize. The

third-place basket isn't big, big, big but still, it's a basket full of all kinds of the best chocolate. Then the third-place ribbon is pinned on Ms. Lee. She smiles, but I think she is wondering who beat her, who finally took her place.

Ms. Howard calls out, "And second place is Miss Ryan Hart!" She says it so fast, no suspense at all, I'm not sure I heard what I think I heard. Not until KiKi yells, "Ryan! Go get your prize."

I walk up and I get the second-place ribbon pinned on me and a big, big basket full of my favorite chocolates. First place goes to Deacon LeRoy for his sweet

potato pie. It's the first time he's entered the contest, too. He is just as shocked as everyone else.

We are asked to stand with each other for a photo. We hold up our baskets and smile at the camera. Deacon LeRoy is to my left, Ms. Lee to my right.

I am in the middle, once again. And standing here doesn't feel bad at all.

CHOCOLATE FOR BREAKFAST

THE NEXT MORNING, I am awake when Dad comes home from work. He tiptoes in just as I am coming back to my bedroom from the bathroom. I go into the living room. "Good morning," I say. I hug him tight and he kisses my forehead.

"You're up early," Dad says. "How was the harvest festival?"

"I won second place in the baking contest," I tell him. I take him by his hand and lead him into the kitchen. "Look at my prize. Amazing, isn't it?"

Dad looks at the basket that's still wrapped in its thick plastic with orange ribbon hanging down and says, "Looks like a whole lifetime of chocolate." He walks over to the sink, washes his hands, and starts making coffee. "I'm surprised you haven't devoured any of it yet."

"I was waiting for you," I tell him. "You taught me how to decorate the cookies and make them look professional. It's your prize, too."

"Well, thank you, Ryan. I guess there's only one thing left to do." Dad unties the ribbon. "Let's celebrate." He takes one of the chocolate bars out and breaks it in half. He hands me my portion.

"But Dad, it's still morning. I haven't even had breakfast."

"It's a special occasion," he says.

Dad drinks coffee and pours me a glass of milk and we eat Moonstruck chocolate for breakfast.

"Our secret," Dad says.

"Promise."

Mom would not be happy about this at all. I start thinking of how to make a case that chocolate for breakfast isn't a bad thing (just in case she finds out, because Mom almost always finds out things I don't want her to know). I think about how sometimes on weekends we have French toast or pancakes for breakfast. How we drizzle the dough in sugary syrup and wash it down with milk. This is just like that, I'll tell her. Something sweet for breakfast.

"Let's play a game," I say.

"Like what?"

"Since it's Halloween weekend, it should be something scary."

"A scary game?"

I think about it. Then I hold up a square of the chocolate bar. "How about, for every piece of chocolate, we have to tell something we're afraid of." Then I say, "You start," because I realize for the first time that I have no idea if Dad has any fears. He's always the one coming to the rescue. I don't know what makes his heart pound, his palms sweat.

"Hmm," Dad says. "I'm scared your mom is going to find out that we're having candy for breakfast."

We laugh.

Dad pops a piece of yumminess in his mouth. "Your turn," he says.

I eat one of my squares. "I'm afraid of big dogs—don't mind puppies, but big ones? No, thank you!"

Dad sips his coffee. "Getting stuck on an elevator," he says as he eats more chocolate.

"Yeah, me too," I tell him. "That would be the absolute worst thing ever."

We take a break from eating the chocolate and Dad tells me about a time he got stuck in an elevator that was on the twenty-ninth floor. "I've never prayed so hard in my life, Ryan." He shakes his head like the memory makes him scared all over again. "Your turn," Dad says.

"Well, don't tell Ray—"

"This whole Scary Chocolate Breakfast is top secret," Dad tells me.

"Okay, so I'm still kind of, sort of scared of the dark. But not like really scared, just a little. Just when it's very dark and quiet and then all of a sudden there's a noise."

"Yeah, living in this old house means there's lots

of random noises. But there's nothing to be afraid of, sweetheart."

"I know." I'm out of chocolate. Dad has one more piece. "You're next," I say.

Dad eats his chocolate slow, takes a sip of coffee, and takes my hand. "I'm afraid moments like this won't happen as you get older."

"What do you mean?" I ask. "I'll never say no to chocolate for breakfast."

"No, what I mean is—well, you're in the fifth grade now. Next year, you'll be in middle school and I . . . I just hope you always remember that your daddy loves you. I know I'm missing out on a lot because of my work schedule, but, well, all this hard work is for you." He squeezes my hand when he says this. And then he says, "Oh, and I'm terrified for any of those boys who will have a crush on you! They'll have to come through me first. And they better be scared."

"Boys? Yuck."

Dad laughs and says, "Good answer, Ryan. Good answer."

The house creaks but I am not afraid because Dad

is with me. He finishes his coffee and I throw away the chocolate wrapper, tying the basket back up like it was before we opened it.

"Happy Halloween, Ryan."

"Happy Halloween, Dad."

That night, before I go to bed, I make a list of all the sweet things I love. At first the list is full of sweet things I can eat: Twix, of course, and hot cocoa, and extra-gooey caramel and marionberry everything, and then I think of all the sweet things that are not food, like my baby sister's smile, Ray's freestyle raps, Mom's hugs, Dad's forehead kisses. Even though everyone is asleep and the sky is dark, and the house is creaking with its nighttime noises, for some reason, I feel less afraid.

GOOD, BETTER, BEST

AT SCHOOL WE are not supposed to have candy, but most of us have brought some of our stashes from Halloween and have it in our pockets or in our backpacks. I'm eating a piece of chocolate from one of the bars that came in my second-prize basket. Just a square at a time so Ms. Anderson doesn't notice. Chocolate is easier to eat quickly. I can let it melt and swallow it before Ms. Anderson even turns around. She is at the board reviewing the science vocabulary we learned last week. She writes a word—*conservation*—on the board and asks, "Who remembers the definition of this word?"

KiKi isn't thinking this candy-sneaking thing through—she is sucking on a hard candy and of all the flavors she could choose, she has chosen cherry, or maybe it's strawberry or watermelon. Whatever it is, it has stained her tongue red and so when she raises her hand to answer Ms. Anderson's question, blurting out, "I know!" I give her a look and shake my head, telling her to stop talking.

KiKi looks at me with a question in her eyes.

I slip my tongue out just enough to give her a hint.

KiKi's eyes get big and she puts her hand down, but it's too late.

Ms. Anderson turns around from the dry-erase board, says, "Next time wait until you're called on, KiKi. But go ahead—what is the definition of the word *conservation?*"

KiKi just stares, not saying anything.

"KiKi, wasn't that you who said *I know?*" Ms. Anderson asks.

KiKi nods.

"Well, go ahead. Tell us the answer."

KiKi doesn't say anything.

"Are you okay?" Ms. Anderson asks. Her face bunches up in confusion.

KiKi nods, even adds her voice this time, moaning, "Uh-huh."

I rescue her because I am finished with my chocolate and I am pretty sure no evidence is on my tongue. "I know the answer!" I blurt out.

"I see we need to do some more work around raising our hands to be called on," Ms. Anderson says. She doesn't call on me since I didn't follow the rules. Instead, she says, "Does anyone know the definition of *conservation and* can raise their hand and wait to be called on?"

Lots of hands rise.

Ms. Anderson calls on Brandon, who says, "*Conservation* means to use something wisely so that you can avoid using it up."

Ms. Anderson turns around and writes the definition on the board, not even thinking that maybe KiKi was up to something.

KiKi mouths a silent *thank you* to me.

We continue on with our science vocabulary and when the bell rings it's time for lunch and recess. "The rain hasn't let up, so we're having an indoor recess today," Ms. Anderson says. "Please go to the gym after you finish eating in the cafeteria."

We line up at the door, me and KiKi straggling behind so we can walk together. KiKi is the caboose of the class, with Ms. Anderson closing the door behind her. Just as I hear the door close, I hear Ms. Anderson whisper, "Oh, and KiKi—I expect you to eat up the rest of your candy before returning to class."

I don't even turn around but I already know KiKi is nodding. Still not opening her mouth, but nodding and nodding and wondering how it is that adults always seem to know.

Indoor recess is never as fun as being outside. Instead of our voices rising in the open sky, they are muffled in this crowded gym and even though it's cold outside, it's hot and stuffy in here. The noise from the bouncing basketballs and the jump ropes slapping the floor echoes off the walls. KiKi and I stop at the board game station and grab Connect Four before anyone else can get it. "Let's sit over there," KiKi says, pointing. She leads the way across the gym and when we get to the corner, she sits down on the floor, crossing her legs. I sit next to her, lean my back against the wall, and stretch my legs out. KiKi goes into her pocket and pulls out two pieces of candy. "Want one?"

"KiKi—you can't just pull those out without checking for adults first. Ms. Anderson is already watching you." I look around the gym to see where the closest teacher is. Ms. Anderson is nearby, but her back is to us because she is watching the group of girls who are double-Dutching, making sure they are taking turns. KiKi discreetly slides the candy into my hand. I look down at it. "And it's blue? We can't eat blue candy right now." I go into my pocket, take out two Moonstruck minis, and give her one. They are bite size and perfect when you just want a little chocolate and don't want to open a whole big bar.

We sit and eat our chocolate and people watch and play Connect Four over and over and over. KiKi beats me every time, except once.

I point to the group of girls double-Dutching. "You sure you don't want to jump rope?" I ask.

"Yeah, I'm sure." KiKi puts in a red checker, blocking me just when I had three black checkers in a row.

Right next to us, Brandon is playing charades

with D, Marcus, and Hannah. I'd much rather be with them—I'm really good at that game. But I don't even ask if KiKi wants to play because I already know the answer. I put my black checker in and as soon as I do I realize the other slot I should have gone for. I look back over at the group playing charades and a memory from two years ago pops into my head. I smile. "Remember when you, me, and Amanda played charades and it took me and you *forever* to guess that Amanda was acting out *woodpecker?*"

KiKi immediately bursts into laughter. "Oh my goodness. Yes, I remember that. I thought she was doing some kind of dance."

"I thought the phrase she was acting out was *neck injury!*"

"Or *bobblehead,*" KiKi says. Her laugh calms slowly until it's completely gone, the way the sun vanishes into the clouds. "You miss Amanda living over here, don't you?"

"A lot," I say. "It would be so fun if she were here right now, wouldn't it?"

When I say this KiKi scoots away from me, just a little, but enough for me to notice. "Is Amanda your best friend?" KiKi asks.

There's that question again.

"Of course," I say. "We're all best friends. Me, you, and Amanda."

"But is she your *best* best friend?" KiKi asks.

My *best* best? "You're both my best friends. We're all best friends," I say again.

"Yeah, but, like, you brought up missing Amanda at the harvest festival and you just said it would be more fun if she was here right now—"

"I said it would *so* fun, not *more* fun." I didn't mean to cut KiKi off, but I want to make sure she knows exactly what I mean.

KiKi's voice gets softer and she isn't looking at me anymore. "I . . . It just makes me feel like maybe Amanda is really your best friend and not me."

I think about all the things Grandma has taught me about love. How it is possible to love many people, many places. "I love you both. I could never choose between the two of you," I tell KiKi. "If I was here with only Amanda right now, I'd wish you were here. I miss the way it was—the three of us always together."

KiKi doesn't say anything.

"Um . . . don't you? Don't you miss the three of us always together?"

"I do. But you really, *really* do."

The bell rings, telling us it's time to go back to class. KiKi and I walk side by side and get in line. Hannah is line leader this week and I stand right behind her. KiKi is behind me.

Ms. Anderson walks over to us and says, "I'll know we're ready once everyone is quiet." She doesn't have to wait long because we've learned our lesson. Last time she had to wait three minutes for the talking and goofing around to stop, so the next day, she shaved three minutes off our lunch time. We had to sit in the classroom in total silence for three whole minutes. It felt like sixty minutes. Sixty very long minutes. And to make it worse, we could hear the other classes being released and walking down the hall to the cafeteria. It was the worst, and I think we all telepathically agreed to never, ever do that again.

When we get back into the classroom it's time to do our math lesson. Right now we're working on fractions and I love it because since I cook and bake a lot, I know a little something about measuring and dividing. I'm trying to focus but it's hard for me to think about numbers right now. All I can think about is KiKi and her question. I have never thought about choosing the *best* of the best. I hope I don't have to.

THE (OTHER) THING ABOUT BEING A BIG SISTER

I AM ROSE'S FAVORITE. EVEN Mom says so. When she is fussy, I know how to get her quiet, and we always end the night with me reading her a bedtime story. Already, she has figured out that Ray is the comedian of the family. When he holds her, he never *just* holds her. He makes faces at her, twisting his lips and scrunching his eyes and nose, trying to make her smile. But she just looks at him, the same way I do.

"She is not amused," I tell Ray. It's a phrase I learned from Grandma. She says it sometimes when she is irritated at a joke that's gone on too long or

when someone thinks they are being funny but aren't. The words drip slowly from her mouth, thick like a bitter cough syrup: *I. Am. Not. Amused.*

"She *is* amused," Ray says. "She likes when I play with her." He sticks his tongue out and what do you know, Rose's tongue slides out as if she is mirroring Ray. I think it's just a coincidence because babies are always sticking their tongues out and making faces, but Ray swears she did it in response to him. "See, told you! She likes this."

"All right," Mom says. "It's time to put Rose back in her crib. She's going to get too spoiled if she's held all the time." Mom takes Rose out of Ray's arms and goes into her room. I follow her. "Ryan, no more holding her till after her nap."

"I know," I say. "I'm just coming in to keep her company."

"She's fine. She doesn't need company right now. It's her nap time."

"Can I read to her until she falls asleep?" I ask. Mom looks like she is about to say no, so I interrupt with my sincerest "Pleeeease?"

"As soon as she's asleep, story time ends and you come out of the room, okay?"

"Promise."

Mom lays Rose in her crib and walks out of the room, leaving the door cracked open just a bit. I start reading and I can hear tiny baby moans and cooing from Rose. I don't even get to the third page of the board book and already, the cooing has stopped. I tiptoe to the crib. Rose is asleep. I whisper to her, "I know I'm your favorite." A smile appears on her face, like she hears and understands what I'm saying. She is always smiling in her sleep. "It's okay, I won't tell Ray."

Now that Rose is napping, I think maybe I can spend time with Mom and start planning our Thanksgiving menu. This year Thanksgiving falls on Grandma's birthday so we're doing something extra special. When I come into the living room, Mom is folding Rose's clothes, making a neat stack of onesies and tiny socks on the sofa cushion next to her. "Four weeks till Turkey Day," I say. "And Grandma's surprise seventieth birthday party! What are we going to do for the menus? Shouldn't we start planning?" I go to the end table and pick up the notepad and pen so I can take notes. "For Thanksgiving, I know Dad's doing our tradition—his smoked turkey—but what sides are we going to make?" I ask. "Oh, and do we have all of the RSVPs for Grandma's surprise party? It's so cool that even her childhood best friend from Georgia is coming." I stop talking just enough to catch my breath, then add, "And do you still want me, Amanda, and KiKi to make desserts? Remember, you said we could make desserts for the party."

"Ryan, we've got time. We can plan it all later." Mom folds a shirt that says *Little Sister* and adds it to the pile. "I'm too tired to think right now." She is yawning and rubbing her eyes and I really don't understand how someone can be too tired to think. All she has to do is name the foods she wants. I'm the one taking notes. I don't push because Mom has that look on her face like she can't take one more thing right now. She finishes folding the clothes, places them in the basket, and leans back. I don't even think it takes her one minute before she falls asleep.

I know Mom is tired because Rose wakes up during the night and has to be fed or sometimes rocked and cradled until she falls back to sleep. I know Mom is tired because since Dad has to work at night, she is the one who is getting up all night long. And since Dad needs his sleep during the day, she is one who is getting up all day long. I know Rose needs a lot of her attention right now, but I really do miss Mom. It is weird to think that, to admit that. How can you miss someone you see every day?

5

RAIN, RAIN

NOVEMBER IS ALWAYS GRAY and rainy. Sometimes there are big storms but most days it's just a constant drizzle and the sky is crying out all her tears. Ray hates the rain. He's been complaining all week because every morning when we're getting ready for school, he asks, "Mom, can I play basketball at Alberta Park with Aiden and Logan after school?"

"It's raining," she always says.

"But the court has a covering."

"Ray, don't ask me again. It'll be raining all week. Come home after school."

"It's always raining. I guess I'm not going to play basketball till May."

I think they're both being extreme. Mom could let Ray go to the park. Ray is right, the court is under a big covering and there's no way he'd come home soaking wet. But Ray is exaggerating when he says he won't be able to play till May. I mean, first of all, he can always play inside at a gym instead of outside, but also, there will be some dry days sprinkled in with the cloudy, rainy ones. The sky isn't always crying. She has her good days, too.

"I hate this time of year," Ray mumbles.

"Ray," Mom says.

And that ends the conversation.

Ray shoves a spoonful of cereal in his mouth.

I keep quiet because I have learned that when the two of them are arguing, it is better for me to mind my own business. But I want to point out to Ray that there's so much to love about this season. My favorite holidays happen this time of year. This month we have Thanksgiving, and this year it's a double-special day because it's also Grandma's birthday, and then Christmas is not too far away, and then New Year's Eve. There's so much to look forward to. Usually on

Thanksgiving, we go to a short prayer and praise service at church. Every year we try to get Grandma to do something special, but she always says, "My gift is having another year on this earth. That's not promised to anyone." We usually honor her wish and don't make too big of a fuss about her birthday, but this year Grandma is getting a whole lot more than prayer and praise. We've been planning a surprise birthday party for her for months. Mom has invited Grandma's best friend, and a few relatives from out of town will be coming, too.

All these celebrations mean more family dinners and dessert, dessert, dessert.

Sweet potato pie, Dutch apple pie, peach cobbler.

Sugar cookies, peanut butter blossom cookies, gingerbread cookies.

Banana pudding, pound cake, chocolate-peppermint cake.

This is the best time of the year!

Winter means days off from school and extra playdates with KiKi and Amanda. Winter means driving around the city to see Christmas lights, going Christmas caroling with the youth choir, and having hot chocolate or hot apple cider to warm me up afterward. This time of year means extra, extra prayers at night: for snow (on a school day so we can stay home and play in it all day long), for the Christmas gifts on my list, for enough money to get gifts for Mom, Dad, and Ray.

I don't know why Ray hates this season so much. There are so many things to love.

🧁

Nothing really good or really bad happens at school today. It is another day of indoor recess and this time me and KiKi join Hannah and D for a game of Uno. KiKi hasn't asked any more questions about being my *best* best friend and I haven't mentioned missing Amanda. I've been thinking about what I want to make KiKi and Amanda for Christmas. Whatever I do, I'll make sure it's the same thing. I don't want KiKi to compare the gifts, thinking one is better than the other.

Grandma picks me up after school and on the way to her house, I bring up planning the menu for Thanksgiving. Grandma is not too tired to think about it. We list our traditional dishes and think of a few new ones to add, too.

"And after Thanksgiving dinner, we'll have to have an extra-special dessert for your extra-special day . . ." I look at Grandma and she looks confused like she has no idea what I'm talking about.

"What am I forgetting, Miss Ryan?"

"Grandma—your birthday!"

"Oh yes, well, that's no cause for doing anything extra. I'll just make my sweet potato pie like usual and maybe a peach cobbler. That'll be plenty of birthday dessert."

"But Grandma, this is a big birthday. Seventy years on this planet. You can't bake your own dessert! Besides, don't you want to celebrate?"

"We'll just do what we always do. I don't want a fuss. Let's keep it simple."

My heart sinks. Grandma wants something simple

and there is nothing simple about a surprise birthday
party with guests being flown to Portland.

Grandma says, "If anyone asks what I want for my
birthday, tell them *nothing*. After we eat Thanksgiving
dinner, I just want an evening of peace and quiet."

My heart drops. Down, down, down.

And it is thumping hard, hard, hard.

How deep can a heart sink?

ME + KIKI + AMANDA

MOM IS BACK TO work at Saturday Market. She's been knitting and sewing for weeks now, getting her winter and holiday merchandise ready. It's chilly today but not raining. Mom says, "I still think you should wear a jacket with a hood. Just in case."

"Okay," I say. Even though I heard the woman on the news say no rain is in the forecast for the whole weekend.

"Have you heard from the girls?" Mom asks. "We can't be late."

"Amanda just called and said that she's two blocks away," I say. "I'll call KiKi now."

For the first time ever, KiKi is coming with us to work a shift at Saturday Market. It's usually only me and Amanda helping my mom, but yesterday I asked KiKi if she wanted to come because I've been thinking of more ways the three of us can do things together. I've been thinking how both KiKi and Amanda are my *best* best.

KiKi and Amanda show up at the same time and after they ooh and ahh over Rose, we leave the house, waving goodbye to Grandma, who is babysitting.

We get to Saturday Market before any shoppers are let in. Vendors are still setting up and a local band is doing their soundcheck on the main stage. When we get to the market, we start setting up on Mom's side of the booth. Ms. Millie is on her side, already set up for the day and ready to go. "Well, I see you brought a new helper today," Ms. Millie says.

"Ms. Millie, this is KiKi," I say.

"Nice to meet you, KiKi. I hope you enjoy the market. If it's as busy as it was last week, I might need one of you to help me out, too," she says.

"Last weekend certainly was busy. Folks getting an early jump on their holiday shopping," Mom says.

Ms. Millie says, "Have you already started shopping for the kids?" Then she looks at me like she's ruined a big secret and says, "I mean, have the kids figured out what they want from Santa?"

I think she says this because she doesn't know if I believe in Santa Claus or not. Mom and Ms. Millie move from talk about Christmas to talk about the new rates for booth rentals. And that leads to whispers about other vendors.

While they gossip, I give myself, KiKi, and Amanda a task to do. I know exactly how Mom likes things set up, so we get started. KiKi is laying out the scarves Mom knitted and I'm placing the matching gloves next to them. Amanda is putting hats on the mannequin head stands. There aren't that many today because last week Mom sold most of them, and with caring for Rose, she didn't have time to make any this week.

All the holiday talk makes me think of what I want for Christmas. "Christmas is a long way away. I wish it was sooner," I say.

"Me too," KiKi says. "I can't wait to see all the gifts under the tree, plus we get a break from school. The best."

Amanda chimes in. "We get a break for Thanksgiving, too. I mean, it's not as long, but at least we get two days off from school."

"But no gifts," KiKi says.

And then I get an idea. "We can get gifts on Thanksgiving. There's no rule that says we have to wait till Christmas."

"Yes, there is. It's called Christmas gifts for a reason," KiKi says.

"Well, yes, but I mean—there's no rule that says we can't start a new tradition and give Thanksgiving gifts. We can have our own Friendship Thanksgiving Day and give each other something that expresses how thankful we are for each other." I wait to see if KiKi and Amanda like this idea. It takes a minute before

Amanda is smiling and nodding and saying she's in. "And the gifts can be simple," I tell them. "Actually, let's make them."

We all agree. Then, KiKi says, "And let's exchange gifts the Friday after Thanksgiving and have a sleepover for the weekend."

"We can do it at my house," Amanda says.

I am even more excited about Thanksgiving. It's not only Grandma's birthday but now it's a special friendship weekend for me, KiKi, and Amanda. This is the best plan ever.

We're all finished setting up, so we sit down on the folding stools and watch the shoppers who are slowly trickling in. Some just look and smile. Others come in and wrap themselves in Mom's thick scarves, looking in the mirror to see if they like them enough to buy them. A few people buy something. Some say, "I'll be back. How long do you stay open?" (Which usually means they will not be back but felt they needed to say something to make Mom feel like there was hope of a sale.)

"So this is it?" KiKi asks. "You two just sit here the whole day?" KiKi sounds so bored, so ready to go.

Amanda says, "Well, we people watch. And sometimes we make up stories about who people are shopping for or how people know each other. We've made up whole stories. Enough to write our own book."

KiKi doesn't seem impressed.

I add, "And sometimes we look around. Remember, this is where I found the missing hairpin that goes with the ones that were left at my house."

"Yeah, I remember. But like—that's it?"

What else did KiKi expect?

Amanda says, "Oh, and we eat. We always get treats from our favorite vendors." She looks at me and says, "We're splitting an elephant ear today, right?"

"Yuck!" KiKi says. I laugh, thinking maybe KiKi doesn't know that elephant ears are delicious funnel cakes, not actual ears. But then she says, "It's just warm dough with too much cinnamon. It's the nastiest thing in the world."

She knows exactly what it is.

"You don't like elephant ears?" I ask. Clearly she doesn't, but I need to ask just to make double sure.

"You do?" KiKi asks, sounding just as shocked. She looks at me and Amanda with disgust all over her face.

Amanda nods. "They are the best. We get one every time we come here."

I can't believe KiKi doesn't like elephant ears. We've been friends our whole lives and somehow I didn't know this. I guess there is always something to learn about a friend, even the friends you know really, really well.

I say, "There are lots of other treats you can get here." And then I remember the snack KiKi loves the most. "I know where we can go. CoolCity Popcorn. They pop it in a huge kettle right in front of you and have unique flavors like salted vanilla and Hawaiian salted caramel."

KiKi stands and pushes her stool under the table. "That sounds amazing. Let's go."

I think I've won her over. Think maybe now she'll

understand why I love coming to Saturday Market. The three of us head over to CoolCity Popcorn. They have hand-twisted pretzels, too, but KiKi is focused on the popcorn. "I'm so glad we can taste test first. It's hard to decide," she says. The three of us taste the original, then the caramel, then the kettle corn. I want to save room for my elephant ear, so I say no thank you when they offer the salted vanilla. "This is the best one!" KiKi says. She orders a small bag. "You sure you don't want to taste?" she asks me and Amanda.

"No, thank you," we both say.

The three of us make our way to my favorite concessions stand. The closer we get, the more I can smell cinnamon and all kinds of goodness in the air. Freshly made elephant ears are being prepared. We forge our way through the crowd and when I turn around, I realize that KiKi is far behind me and Amanda. Amanda doesn't hear me when I say, "Hold on, we need to wait for KiKi!" So now she's already at the stand probably wondering where me and KiKi are.

I have stopped in the middle of this enormous crowd to wait for KiKi and now people are bumping into me, rolling their eyes, accidentally stepping on my feet. I am in the way. Finally, KiKi catches up. "Oh my goodness," she says. "There are so many people here. I can't believe you come here every weekend. It's too much." KiKi is back to complaining and all I want is for her to see why I love coming to the market. All I want is for her to love it, too.

Amanda and I get our elephant ear and split it in half to share. I hold mine in the napkins I grabbed and I don't take one bite until we find a spot to sit. I want to savor every bite and if I eat it all while walking, I'll hardly enjoy it. We find open space on the cement steps near the fountain. The trolley makes its way along the track and behind us there's a man playing bucket drums and singing. I take my first bite and the warm dough is soft and sweet and buttery and cinnamon-ey. And perfect (no matter what KiKi says).

Amanda eats her half so quickly, I barely see her take a bite. I am in the middle of her and KiKi, so when she talks she leans over me to make sure KiKi can hear. "Isn't this the best?" Amanda says.

KiKi zips her hoodie. "I guess. I mean—yes, it's, it's

just . . . not what I expected. I'm having fun, though."
KiKi is not good at hiding how she feels. She is not into
this. At all. "It's kinda cold," she says as she puts her
hands in her pockets. Her popcorn is long gone now.

"At least it's not raining," I say. Trying to get her to
see that it could be worse.

"True," she says.

We sit and people watch under Portland's cloudy, gray sky, our bellies full of the market's best eats. KiKi leans her head on my shoulder and Amanda scootches closer to me to make room for a little girl who is climbing the stone. I know KiKi isn't having the best of times, but I'm glad she came. At least we're all together.

7

MOM & ME

MONDAY MORNINGS ALWAYS BRING a chance to start over, to refocus. At least, that's what Ms. Anderson says. Every Monday, she starts the week off by saying, "And how will we be better this week?" It isn't a question for us to answer out loud, but one for us to think about. This week I'm going to try to be better at ignoring Brandon, who spent all last week making up raps about my name. He thinks he's so funny, but most of the class doesn't even laugh at him, except for Marcus, who laughs at everything. He has more giggles than words, always. The only time I really hear Marcus talk is when we have our read aloud circles. But mostly, he is a laughing mime—shoulders shaking, mouth wide, big smile across his face.

Today, it is taking extra, extra focus to ignore Brandon, who keeps asking me, "Ryan, what's your middle name?"

He's asking because Ms. Anderson just passed a handout that has a black and white photo on it and the name Thelma Johnson Streat under it. "Hey, she has a weird last name like Ryan," Brandon says. He thinks it's strange that Thelma Johnson Streat has two last names, and of course he's making a big deal about her last name being spelled *S-T-R-E-A-T* instead of *S-T-R-E-E-T*. "Thelma Johnson Streat spells her name wrong just like Ryan *H-A-R-T* does. What is with weird last names and spelling them wrong?" Brandon laughs and his miming shadow laughs, too.

Ms. Anderson doesn't even hear him when he says it and I really don't understand how he's so good at saying things loud enough for me to hear and quiet enough that she doesn't.

Ms. Anderson says, "We are watching a documentary about Thelma Johnson Streat and I want you to take notes on the back of the handout. There are sentence starters to guide your note taking."

I turn the paper over. It looks like a Mad Libs sheet with sentences that start off and end with blank lines. The movie begins and already I love this woman, Thelma Johnson Streat. She was the first Black woman to have a painting included in MoMA's permanent collection. And her work is permanently showcased at the Smithsonian National Museum of African American History and Culture in Washington, DC.

She grew up right here in Portland, Oregon, and went to Washington High School. The school closed in 1981 but the building is still standing, and now what used to be the auditorium is a performance hall where singers and musicians have concerts. The classrooms are office spaces for local businesses.

These are the things I am writing down in my notes when Brandon sings my name, "Ryyaaan . . .

oh, Ryyaaan. What's your middle name? You can tell me. I promise I won't tease you."

I ignore him.

"Is it a name that should be a last name?"

I just keep looking straight ahead.

"Is it another body part? Ryan Eye Hart? Ryan Knee Hart?"

Nothing from me.

"Come on, you can tell me," Brandon says again.

To shut him up, I yell, "I don't even have a middle name, so shut up and leave me alone!"

So much for starting this week off being and doing better.

Ms. Anderson comes over to my desk and says, "Ryan, I need you to stop talking. Focus on the film."

"But I am focusing!" I show Ms. Anderson my handout so she can see my notes.

"You can't focus and talk at the same time," she says.

"But I was focusing. I wasn't talking, I was just telling Brandon to leave me alone."

"So, you were talking?"

"But only to tell him—"

"Ryan, whatever you need to tell him can wait. Watch the movie." Ms. Anderson walks away. She has a way of ending a conversation even when you want to say more.

I can't believe I am the one getting the talking-to when it's Brandon who was being disrespectful. I can't believe I let him get to me and gave him a response. I think at least now that he knows I don't have a middle name, he'll leave me alone and stop asking me about it. Especially since I've told him to shut up (which I know I should not have said, but he really does need to stop talking to me. Forever).

What do you know, Brandon makes an even bigger deal out of me not having a middle name. "Ryan No-Middle-Name Hart," he says. "Everyone has a middle name. Why don't you?"

"Because Ryan is a strong enough name on its own!" I answer.

Ms. Anderson pauses the movie and says, "Ryan,

would you like to tell the class what is so important that it can't wait?"

No, I would not.

I would like Brandon to leave me alone and I would like to learn how to whisper because clearly I talk too loud, since my voice is the only voice Ms. Anderson ever hears.

Hannah comes to my rescue. "It's Brandon. He keeps teasing her about her name," she says.

I look at Hannah and tell her *thank you* with only my eyes.

Ms. Anderson says, "Brandon and Ryan, I'll need you to stay seated when I dismiss the class for lunch."

Brandon explodes in a bunch of huffing and puffing and "But I didn't do anything!" and "This isn't fair." Even though he absolutely did do something and this is absolutely fair.

I hide my smile because I know it would be strange for me to start smiling at a time like this. But I am kind of happy because for once, for once, Brandon is getting in trouble. And besides, I don't really care about being late to lunch. It's an indoor recess day anyway because it's raining.

Once the class is dismissed for lunch, Ms. Anderson closes her door and says to me and Brandon, "I'm having your lunch brought to the classroom, and you two can sit together in here and eat since you like to talk to each other so much."

Brandon says, "And after we eat, can we be dismissed for recess?"

Ms. Anderson walks over to the bookshelf at the back of the room. "I have a better idea," she says. She grabs two books and sets them down in the middle of our table. Ms. Anderson has a smirk on her face like she thinks she's really laying it on thick. Like this will teach us a lesson. Like reading is the ultimate punishment.

If only she remembered how much I love books. Especially on rainy days.

When I get home from school, Mom stops me at the door, says, "Don't take your coat off. Me and you are going shopping." She already has her coat on and her purse hanging off her shoulder.

"Shopping?"

"Yes, I noticed your shoes this morning when you were leaving. You need a new pair. Those are worn out. I'm surprised they're still comfortable."

Well, they aren't that comfortable anymore, but I haven't said anything because I know we don't have a lot of money to buy new shoes. The only reason I got new clothes at the start of the school year is because Grandma helped out.

Mom says, "Those won't hold up much longer in the rain. You need a new pair before the sole gets any holes. I thought you and I could have some mommy-daughter time, get a treat at the mall's food court and then do some shopping."

The best thing about this is that baby Rose is not in Mom's arms, which means she is not coming with us. I love her, but I am glad that today will be just me and Mom. Not even Ray is coming.

We say goodbye to Dad, who is feeding Rose from a bottle. Mom kisses him on his cheek, says, "I'll be back in enough time for you to get in a nap before you leave."

"Have fun," he says.

When we get into the car, Mom asks me what I want to listen to. This *is* a special day—Mom hardly likes the music I like, so letting me choose is a big deal. But we don't listen to the music because for the whole ride, Mom is asking me about how school is, what my favorite subject is, what's challenging. I tell her all the good things but don't let her know about Brandon and how I had to stay in at recess. I figure, this is mommy-daughter time, why ruin it with talking about how I got in trouble at school. Instead, I tell Mom all I learned about Thelma Johnson Streat.

Mom gets so excited as she listens to me. She tells me, "I am so glad Ms. Anderson is teaching you this history. I didn't learn about Thelma Johnson Streat till I was in college."

"Were you taking an art class?" I ask.

"No, actually, I was taking a dance course."

"Why were you learning about a visual artist in a dance class?"

"Well, people can be many things. Thelma Johnson Streat had a lot of talents. She loved dance and she also loved to travel. She created choreography inspired by the many places she visited. I think it was sometime in the 1940s when she had a big performance at the San Francisco Museum of Art. She showed off dances she made up, choreography that combined African, Haitian, Native American, Hawaiian, and Portuguese dance forms."

We stop at a light and I look out the window, able to see all the cars and license plates I want because I am sitting on Ray's side and I am not in the middle of anyone, so nothing is blocking my view.

Mom says, "What I loved learning about Thelma Johnson Streat is that she performed dances, songs, and folktales from around the world to bring people together and to show the beauty that lies in all cultures." The light changes and we continue on Martin Luther King Jr. Boulevard. Mom says, "You know how your father and I are always telling you to be who we named you to be? That you come from a people who paved the way for us to be here, that we want you to make them—and us—proud?"

"Yes, I know. I remember."

"Thelma Johnson Streat is one of those people. There are so many others."

Our first stop at the mall is Joe Brown's Caramel Corn. We buy a box of caramel and cheese popcorn mixed together, eat a few handfuls, then make our way to get shoes.

We spend the rest of the evening walking through the mall, stopping at stores, with Mom pointing and saying, "What about these?" and almost always I ask if we can keep looking. All the shoes she is pointing to are either too clunky or too boring, and always too ugly.

Finally, we find a pair that I like and there's only one box left in my size. I practically leap out of my shoes to free my feet so I can try them on. Mom says, "Wait, Ryan. I need to check the price." I can tell by the look on her face that these shoes that I just got so excited about trying on are out of our budget. Mom says, "Hold on," and walks over the store clerk. "Excuse me, sir. Do you have anything similar to this style but a little less expensive?"

"Let's see," the man says. His hair is dyed a bright green and the front keeps falling in his face. He moves it back in place and says, "Come with me." We walk to the back of the store. A big sign reads *Clearance*. "You should be able to find something here," he says. "In fact, I think last season's pair was returned and I'm pretty sure we marked them down. It's a different color and I'm not sure if it's the same size you're looking for, though."

"We don't mind a different color," Mom says.

We follow him and the whole time I am wishing and wishing, *Please, please, please let them be in my size and let them be a color I like.*

He walks us to the row that has my size. And I search all the boxes for something similar to the sneakers I want. It's not neat back here like at the front of the store. I look and look, and then Mom says, "Ryan, here they are! I found them." She holds up sneakers that are the exact same as the ones I love but instead of pink and gray, they are purple and gray.

"I think I like these better," I say.

Mom looks relieved, like she had been praying, too. "Okay, try them on. Let's make sure they're a good fit."

I try them on and then Mom makes me walk around the store to make sure they feel good. "Yep, they feel great," I tell her. I say it so loud, the woman shopping across the aisle from us turns and smiles at me like she knows there is nothing like a cute pair of brand-new shoes that fit perfectly.

When we get to the counter to pay, the cashier rings up the shoes and says, "Well, it must be your lucky day. There's an extra discount on top of the first discount."

"Our lucky day, indeed." Mom exhales and takes out her wallet. She pays for the shoes and I am feeling thankful that she didn't have to spend too much money on me today. I will take the best care of these shoes because I'm not sure when she'll have enough to buy another pair.

We leave the mall and just when we are close to the house, driving past Alberta Park, Mom pulls over and parks. "I have an idea," she says. "Why don't you come up to the front seat so we can finish our popcorn. You know if we bring it in the house, we'll have to share with Ray and your dad."

I take my seat belt off and get to the front seat as fast as I can. Mom and I eat our treat till the very last kernel.

NEW (OLD) SHOES

THE NEXT DAY IT is raining—no, not raining: it is storming. The rain is the drenching kind, not a sprinkle or tap-tap-tap. Water is gushing out from the sky. The first thing I think is, *Ugh! Another indoor recess day.* And then I think about my new shoes. I wanted to wear them today, but I don't want to wear them in this rain. I know that eventually I'll have to get them wet and dirty, but not the first time wearing them. They deserve at least one day of being dry. I'll have to wait for another day. It doesn't even have to be a dry day, just not a Noah's Ark kind of storm.

KiKi's mom is dropping me, Ray, and KiKi off at

school. As soon as I step outside to get in the car, I feel a stream of water enter my left shoe. I didn't even know there was a hole in the sole. How did that happen? When did that happen? It's too late to turn around and this is the most I'll be outside, so I just get in the car so we're not late for school.

Walking from the car to the inside of the school, my left foot gets even more wet. When we step inside the building, Ray runs off to join Aiden and Logan. I make sure I wipe my shoes on the thick mat that is at the door to soak up all our wet, muddy feet. KiKi stomps on the mat, shakes herself dry, and is already taking her coat off even though we haven't made it to our classroom yet.

The hallway is crowded with students rushing in out of the rain and heading to class. As I walk on the linoleum floor there's a squeaky noise every time I put my left foot down. With each step there's a squeak and a whistle. Squeak, whistle, squeak, whistle. No matter how much I try to adjust the way I walk so the noise will stop. Squeak, whistle, squeak, whistle.

And here comes Brandon, who seems to watch every move I make. He asks me, "Why are you walking funny?"

I don't want a repeat of yesterday, so I don't say anything. I just keep walking like I don't hear him. But then KiKi notices and says, "Are your sneakers squeaking? I think you need to wipe them off again."

I walk back to the door and stomp my feet and drag them along the mat. But it doesn't work. My left shoe is making noise like one of Rose's toys. Brandon starts laughing and his shadow starts, too.

I yell at them, "Laugh all you want to, but tomorrow I'm coming to school with the best shoes you've ever seen. I have new shoes at home that I just didn't want to wear today, but just wait until tomorrow." I walk away fast so I can hurry up and get away from them. I get into the classroom, squeaking and whistling the whole time, and sit at my desk.

I try not get out of my seat again.

The next day I wake up before anyone else. I could hardly sleep thinking about wearing my new shoes and showing them off to all my classmates. No squeaking and whistling today. And no rain, either. As soon as KiKi sees me, she says right away, "You were right about the shoes. I really like them."

"Thanks," I say.

We walk into the school building, not needing to take extra time at the mat today. KiKi whispers, "And I'm sorry for bringing attention to your shoes yesterday. I wasn't trying to embarrass you or—"

"I know, it's okay," I tell her. "Doesn't even matter anymore."

It takes a while for people to notice my new shoes, but at lunch the compliments start pouring in. On my way back from taking my trash to the garbage, Hannah says—loud so the whole table can hear— "Ryan, I love your shoes. Those are so cute." Hannah is one of the best dressed at Vernon, so it's kind of a big deal that she approves of what I'm wearing.

Then someone else says, "I love them, too. Where'd you get them?"

"If the Shoe Fits at NorthSide Mall," I say.

And then Brandon looks down at my feet, then back up at me. "My sister used to have a pair like that. She took them back, though, because—" Brandon stops midsentence. Maybe it's because I give him a look, a pleading look, that says *not today, please not today.* Or maybe it's because even he is tired of picking on me. I'm not sure why he stops with his story—a story that I think is about how his sister took the shoes back either because they were too tight, or too big, or too ugly. I just don't want anyone knowing that I have hand-me-down, returned, bought-on-clearance shoes. Brandon clears his throat. "Oh, wait. Those aren't the same," he says. "My mistake." Our eyes catch and he kind of smiles at me—an actual smile from Brandon. He says, "But the ones my sister got—the ones she took back, I'm the one who picked them out. She didn't like them, but I thought they looked pretty cool."

The bell rings and Ms. Anderson lines us up so we can get back to class.

MORE THAN ENOUGH

VERNON ELEMENTARY IS HAVING a canned food drive, so I am standing on a step stool searching the kitchen pantry for soups to donate. The class with the most cans will win an ice-skating party. I've always wanted to go ice-skating. I think it would be so fun to go with my whole class. I bet KiKi would be really good at it because she's good at dancing and moving her body like a beautiful, graceful swan. I'll probably fall a whole lot, but that'll be fun, too.

"What are you looking for?" Mom asks.

I didn't hear her come into the kitchen. "Looking for canned food to donate for our school drive."

"You need to ask before you just go giving away our food." Mom isn't yelling at me, but her voice sounds angry, annoyed. I don't understand why she is upset. She's the one who is always telling me *be who we named you to be, be a leader, be kind.* And here I am trying, but all she does is fuss at me.

Parents are the most confusing people on the planet.

"Mom, I have to give something. I can't be the only one in my class who doesn't bring a donation."

Mom comes over to the cabinet and takes a can of chicken noodle soup out of my hands. "We need these," she tells me. She stretches her neck like an ostrich and looks into the back of the pantry. "Ryan, I . . . there's nothing we can afford to give this time. I just bought these groceries and they need to last."

When she says this, I feel tears rising inside of me but I push them back down. I thought Mom was just fussing for no good reason, but what she's saying is we don't have anything to spare. There was a time, before Dad lost his old job, when we had more than enough, but now we have just enough.

Mom looks like she is pushing down tears, too. She inhales a deep breath. Breathes in, out. "I . . . let me see . . ." She keeps looking and looking and moving cans around, then she pulls out two cans of tuna. "You can give these." Mom helps me down from the step stool. "I love that you are so generous, Ryan. I didn't mean to raise my voice at you. Just . . . just make sure you ask first before you go giving things away, okay? We're on a tight budget. Everything is accounted for." Mom kisses me on my forehead. "Leave it to you to remind me that there's always something to give." She folds the step stool and puts it away. Mom walks out of the kitchen, repeating herself over and over, not really talking to me anymore. "There's always something to give . . . always something to give."

At dinner, we all sit at the dining room table eating warmed-up leftovers—meatloaf and oven-roasted potatoes. Rose is in her baby bouncer, right next to Mom's chair. Ray is what Grandma calls *a chatterbox*—talking nonstop and not letting anyone else get a word in. He is all excited about winning the citywide poetry slam. "So now I get to enter the regional competition and that's happening in Seattle and—"

As he talks, Rose is making noise like she is talking, too. And the more Ray talks, the louder Rose babbles.

Ray says, "Hey, Rose, it's my turn. I'm the one sharing right now."

But that just makes Rose babble louder.

Everyone is laughing (except Ray). I am laughing the hardest. "It's like she knows you're trying to tell us a story and is refusing to let you talk."

Rose is quiet when I say this, but as soon as Ray starts up again, she coos and gurgles loud.

Ray tries again. "Seattle sounds so fun. I can't wait to—"

Shriek! Rose gives a high-pitched yell like she is saying "Enough!" Or maybe she is excited for Ray and is cheering him on. I'm not sure. All I know is it is a competition between the two of them and Rose is going to get the last word—or in this case, the last sound.

Ray bends and hovers over Rose's bouncer. "You got something to say? Huh? Go ahead."

Nothing.

Rose is completely silent.

Ray waits and waits.

Silence from Rose.

Ray continues his story. "Okay, so I've got to write the best verse I've ever written. I mean, this is—"

Shriek! Rose is at it again.

Now even Ray is laughing. We all are. And none of us can stop.

We normally get in trouble for doing too much laughing at the dinner table, but I guess Ray and I can't get in trouble if Mom and Dad are tickled, too. Mom is laughing so hard, her eyes are watery. Those tears she pushed down earlier are releasing, releasing.

Mine are, too.

Tears of joy. That's something I hope we never run out of.

COOKING LESSONS

AMANDA INVITED ME AND KiKi over to spend the day at her house. Well, not just me and KiKi—Red is here, too. I haven't seen her since camp. Even though we had our not-so-good moments, I do think she really meant it when she said *sorry*, so I'm okay with her being with us today. Amanda asked me and KiKi if it was okay with us for Red to come, so at least I had a say and wasn't surprised to see her when I got here. Amanda asked if I could teach everyone how to make something yummy, so we're making applesauce. Her mom bought all the ingredients I asked for. Actually, she bought way more than what I asked for. The kitchen looks like they are opening their own produce stand. Amanda says, "Ryan, are you ready to teach us?"

"Yes," I say. I wash my hands and dry them on the hanging towel. "Okay, so my grandma taught me how to make two kinds of applesauce last fall. It's so simple—not that many ingredients at all."

Amanda's older sister, Melissa, who helped get everything prepped for us, is sitting in the living room, supposedly keeping an eye on us, but mostly she is on her phone. Their little sister, Zoe, is with their mom at a playdate.

The kitchen and living room are one big space, no wall closing one room off from the other. The kitchen is so big that all four of us can fit without bumping into each other. At my house, our hips and arms would be knocking into one another like bumper cars. Amanda doesn't even know how amazing this kitchen is. She doesn't cook, so she doesn't get it, but the farmer's sink, the chef's stove with dual fuel range, the marble island that seats eight—this is the perfect kitchen to cook in. I'll come over any day to teach her a recipe.

Me, KiKi, Amanda, and Red huddle in our cook's circle and I give directions. "Since we're making two kinds of applesauce and there are four of us, let's split into two groups. Amanda and Red, KiKi and me."

KiKi looks relieved when I say this. Like she feels special that I chose her. She hasn't brought up being my *best* best friend in a while, but just now, the look in her eyes tells me she is still thinking about it.

"We have to peel the apples and dice all the fruit. Then we'll put them in the pots with about three-fourths of a cup of water and let them cook until they are soft."

Red asks, "Who's making the strawberry batch?"

"Um . . . you and Amanda."

Red smiles. "I've never had strawberry apple-sauce."

KiKi says, "Me neither."

Amanda eats one of the strawberries. "It's so good. Sweet and tart and delicious."

"And they will taste even better once we blend them with the apples because we're using the sweetest apples, Pink Lady, Honeycrisp, and McIntosh," I tell them.

We get to peeling and cutting and once we're finished with that, we put the fruit in the pots. I instruct them like this is my very own cooking class. "Turn the burner down to simmer."

The apples and strawberries smell so good. Even Melissa is asking when it will be ready. KiKi asks, "When do I add the cinnamon?"

I poke the apples with a fork and say, "In about two minutes. And then we'll add a little bit of honey, too."

I love teaching them something I know how to do.

Amanda says, "This is so pretty. The strawberries turned the apples pink."

"Test it to see if it's soft enough to smash," I say.

Once the apples and strawberries are ready, we

turn the stove off and set the pots aside to cool. "Red, can you set the timer for fifteen minutes? We have to let the fruit cool before we smash and jar it."

We wait and wait and finally the timer dings. Now, we can smash the fruit so we can finally eat our applesauce. There's only one potato masher. KiKi uses it and Amanda uses an oversized fork for their batch. I tell them, "Some people use a food processer or blender to make it extra smooth, but I like it kind of chunky."

When we're finished mashing everything together, we spoon the applesauce into sealable jars—enough for people to have their very own serving. We clean the kitchen and then sit at the island and eat.

KiKi takes a bite. "This. Is. So. Good."

"See, I told you," Amanda says.

"I didn't even know how good applesauce could be. I like it chunky like this," Red says. "And it's still a little warm. So good."

We each have a little of both flavors and now the kitchen is quiet again, but this time it's only because our mouths are full. After we finish eating, KiKi's

mom picks us up and we ride home to the other side of town.

As soon as I get home, I write about this day in my memory journal. I write about how the four of us were able to spend the day together and no one got their feelings hurt, how we worked together to make the most delicious snack, how we scraped our jars till there was nothing left. This is a memory I never want to forget. I am already excited about going back to Amanda's for our Friendship Thanksgiving sleepover. I think about how much fun we are going to have and decide that for our cooking lesson, I'll teach them a holiday recipe. Maybe we'll make my award-winning sugar cookies. I'll never admit it to anyone, but I'm glad Red won't be there. Spending time with her today was fine, but it will be nice to just have me, KiKi, and Amanda together like old times.

I think about KiKi asking who is my *best* best friend and I wonder what Amanda would say if I asked her that question. She sure does like having Red around. Maybe she feels the same way I do about her and KiKi. It's impossible to choose. Maybe some questions are better off not being asked.

♠

It's Sunday afternoon and Grandma and Mr. Simmons have come over for Sunday dinner. The food has been devoured and now it's time for dessert. Grandma and I are in the kitchen cutting into the chocolate spice cake that I made. Mom is in her bedroom putting Rose to sleep and Ray is in the living room with Dad and Mr. Simmons watching a football game. The TV is so loud, I can hardly hear Grandma's soft voice. I stand closer to her so I can hear her better. "You made this all by yourself?" she asks.

"Yes," I tell her. "It's a really rich chocolate cake with cinnamon, allspice, and ground cloves to add a holiday taste to it."

Grandma cuts a thin slice and puts it on her plate.

I try not to stare at her while she tastes it, but it's hard because I want to know if she likes it, and the way you know if Grandma likes something you've

cooked is if she leans her head back and closes her eyes with the first bite. She sits down at the kitchen table and takes her first bite.

Head back, eyes closed.

Grandma says, "Ryan, you've outdone yourself. This is really, really good. I think I could eat this every day." She takes another bite. "Remember when I said that I didn't want anything special for my birthday?"

"Yes, I remember."

"Well, I've changed my mind. I want you to bake me your chocolate spice cake. That's it."

"What do you mean *that's it*?" I ask, hoping maybe Grandma changed her mind about only wanting a day of peace and quiet.

"That's what I want for my birthday. Just cake and rest."

I promise Grandma that I will make her this same exact cake. But I don't promise her anything else.

True Friends

I'M SPENDING THE WEEKEND at Grandma's. It's part sleepover, part work time for me. She has a list of chores that she's paying me to do, and when I'm finished we're going to watch a movie. She promised I could stay up as late I want, so maybe we'll watch two (even though I think Grandma might fall asleep before we even finish the first one). Grandma hands me her notebook and points to the list she wrote. The list isn't bad at all: dusting, sweeping, mopping, taking out the trash, and sorting through a big bin of paper and junk mail to shred in her shredder. "Now, you don't have to do everything on this list. Just pick what you wish and I'll pay you accordingly."

"But can I do everything on the list?" I ask. "I need all the money I can get, so I can get the materials to make Kiki's and Amanda's special friendship gifts." I tell Grandma about my new tradition with KiKi and Amanda.

"That's a beautiful thing to do," Grandma says.

I get to work and just as I am finishing shredding papers, Grandma says, "When you're done with that, come on in here and help me with something."

I finish up and go into Grandma's bedroom. She is folding the fresh laundry she's taken out of the dryer, but instead of putting the clothes in her drawers or closet, she is packing them in bags. "Grandma, you have a lot of clothes."

"This is why I am giving so many away. It's time to purge. I'll be donating these to a shelter."

Grandma's room smells like lavender because she left the dryer sheets in the clothes baskets. But besides all the freshness, I smell rose water, too. Grandma's favorite perfume. As we fold and bag the clothes, I look around Grandma's room. I am hardly ever in here, so it feels special sitting on her queen bed. Grandma's walls are bare but she has an over-sized dresser against the wall on the opposite side. On top of the dresser, there are photos of the family. I even see a few of me and Ray. My favorite is the big photo of Grandma in the middle of them all. She is much younger in the photo and instead of her hair being straight, it is in an Afro. "Grandma, you look so strong and beautiful in that picture." I jump off the bed and walk over to the dresser to get a better look.

"Thank you. I love that photo, too. It's the day I met your grandfather. He took that picture when I wasn't looking." Grandma points to another frame, right beside her Afro picture. "And I love that one, too. That's me and my friend Charlotte Holmes when I still lived in Valdosta, Georgia. Can you believe I've known her most of my life? That's a long, long time to have a friend."

I think of KiKi and Amanda when Grandma says this. Then I wonder if this is the friend Mom invited to Grandma's surprise party. I investigate. "When's the last time you've seen Ms. Holmes?"

"Oh my. I can't even recall. Years . . . many years. The older we both get, the less we travel. Portland is a long way from Valdosta."

"Wouldn't it be nice to see her soon?" I ask. I'm not trying to give it away, but I think maybe if she gets it on her mind how much she misses her friend, she'll be happy about the surprise and forgive me for keeping a secret from her.

"Well, we talk all the time. A few times a week. Nothing can break up a true friendship," Grandma tells me. "You always find a way to stay connected to the people you love."

"Is Ms. Holmes your best friend?" I ask. I walk over to the bed, start back up with the folding and packing. I tell Grandma what KiKi asked about being my *best* best, how I don't think I could ever choose.

Grandma says, "I like to think of Charlotte as my *true* friend. Not my best friend. I have more than one true friend—people I can trust, people who care about me. Those friends aren't perfect, they're not the best at all times—and neither am I—but our love is real. Our friendship is *true*."

"I like that," I tell Grandma. "KiKi and Amanda are my *true* friends. That's better than best."

When Mom comes to pick me up the next day, she thanks Grandma for giving me spending money. Grandma hands me an envelope and says what she always says when she pays me for doing chores. "I didn't give it to her, she earned it. I really appreciate all the help."

We say our goodbyes and Mom drives us home. I am in the back seat counting the money I earned. Grandma gave me extra. I'll definitely have enough to get what I need to make my Thanksgiving gifts. I can't wait till I go back to Saturday Market. For once, I'll be buying more than elephant ears.

AXELS & TWISTS

THE REST OF THE weekend goes by too fast. It is already Monday and I'm back to school. Ms. Anderson begins the day with a special announcement. "I am happy to announce that our fall field trip will be to the NorthSide Mall ice-skating rink!"

The class cheers.

"If any of your parents or caretakers want to come with us as chaperones, please have them check the box on the bottom of the permission slip." Ms. Anderson walks around the room passing out the slips.

I fold the paper, put it in my pocket. I know Mom

won't be able to chaperone, but when I get home, I'm going to tell Dad about the field trip. He keeps talking about missing out on things and worrying that in middle school, I'll be too busy for quality time. Maybe he'll give up a few hours of sleep to ice-skate with me and chaperone my class. I don't get my hopes up too high. I know he needs his rest, but it doesn't hurt to ask.

Even though the NorthSide skating rink is in my neighborhood, I rarely see people who look like me skating. I think about this as we ride the school bus to the mall. I wonder what it's going to be like. Not just the skating, but the staring and snickering that sometimes happen when I come into a place that feels like I don't belong. Maybe since we're such a big group, we'll have the whole rink to ourselves. That would be the best. Just us kids from Vernon and our chaperones with a whole magical ice playground to ourselves.

When the bus pulls up to the mall, Dad says, "You ready to have fun?"

"Ready!" I say.

He's been coaching me ever since I invited him, telling me how to move on the ice so I don't fall, how to balance myself, how to stride. Dad is good at skating. When he was a teenager, he played hockey in a community league, so he's kind of a pro.

Once we get inside the mall, get our skates, and get on the ice, I realize that we are the only ones here. There are people in the mall—mostly elderly people or moms pushing strollers—but there's no one else on the ice. There's a sign that says CLOSED FOR PRIVATE EVENT: WELCOME VERNON OWLS. I feel special knowing they made a sign just for us. An abundance of mistletoe hangs over the rink, cascading above our heads, blowing us kisses.

Some of the shoppers stand on the outside of the rink and watch us, which makes me more nervous. I am holding Dad's hand, inching my way around the rink. I am grabbing him so tight, my knuckles hurt.

This is one of the scariest things I've ever done—even scarier than public speaking—but it's also so, so fun.

"You're okay, you're okay," Dad keeps telling me. "I got you."

Like I thought, KiKi is in the middle of the rink doing all kinds of twists and turns. Her long legs gliding and lifting. "Come out here," she yells.

"No way." I like it right here by the wall. Just in case I start to fall, I'll be able to reach out and grab on to it.

Dad says, "Let's go. I'm not going to let you fall. And if you do, guess what?"

"What?"

"You'll just get back up." He smiles like it's all so simple. But falling in front of my friends won't be anything to smile about.

"Okay," I say. "But let's go extra slow."

We skate out to the middle of the rink to join KiKi and Hannah. I wobble, wobble my way but then start feeling more confident once I realize how far out I've come without falling—or even almost falling.

Dad says, "All right, we'll have to stop soon. You'll like this—we're about to make snow! Bring your feet together, bend your knees and glide, now slide your foot out forward and diagonally."

Dad is right, we put so much pressure on our skates while stopping that the blades kick up ice and make it look like snow on the rink. We form a circle and KiKi says, "I can show you some turns."

I am reluctant, but then I decide to try. I came here to have fun today. I can't hug the wall and hold Dad's hand the whole time.

Once Dad sees I am comfortable, he says, "I'm going to go over there and check on some of the fellas." He points to Brandon, his shadow Marcus, and D.

KiKi does something so fancy that both Hannah and I look at each other and start laughing. Hannah shakes her head back and forth over and over. "Absolutely no way I can do that. You're doing axel jumps like this is the Olympics. We need level one, KiKi."

"Yeah, something simple," I say.

KiKi smiles. "Sorry—okay, let me think." She balances herself, bending her knees just a little. KiKi is naturally good at so many things. Sometimes I don't think she realizes she's talented, that everyone can't do what she does.

I say, "I hardly know what I'm doing out here. How about we just skate in circles for a while and I can practice turning and gliding."

"I like that plan," Hannah says.

We hold hands and move on the ice. The first time around the rink, I'm a little wobbly and I fall, bringing KiKi down with me. But then I relax, get into a rhythm, and the next time I go around smooth like I've been doing this for a while.

We pass by Dad, who is skating with the boys. He's teaching them a few skating tricks. Brandon shows off but then he falls and slides across the ice. He laughs and tries to play it off, saying, "I did that on purpose," when we all know he's just clumsy. Dad helps him up and I want to tell him not to help the boy who is always teasing me, but I don't say anything. I just keep going around and around in circles with KiKi and Hannah.

Then one of my favorite songs blares out of the

speakers and echoes over our heads. KiKi and Hannah start singing and I start dancing and the whole class comes to the middle of the rink, slipping and sliding, and singing and dancing. Even Ms. Anderson has joined us. She's with Dad and the rest of the parent chaperones showing off old-school moves.

We spend the afternoon laughing and singing and twisting and spinning and bumping into each other and getting back up to do it all over again, and again.

Our blades, like pens, writing on the ice, tiny scribbles, leaving our mark.

CHANGE OF PLANS

AFTER THE SCHOOL BUS ride back to Vernon, Dad drives me and KiKi home. KiKi and I are sitting in the back seat and all of a sudden she has a cloud of gloom hovering over her like we didn't just have the best time ever. "What's wrong?" I ask.

KiKi talks low, as if she doesn't want Dad to hear her. I don't think he's paying attention to what we are saying. He is singing along with the radio, listening to the station that plays old-school jams—the songs from his high school years. "I, um, I have to tell you something," KiKi says.

"What's wrong?"

"Um, so . . . well, you know how Vernon goes up to

eighth grade and if students want to stay at Vernon for middle school, they can?"

"Of course I know that. What's wrong?"

"Well, my mom thinks I should enroll in a school that just has grades sixth through eighth. So I might not be at Vernon with you for middle school."

"But KiKi, we've gone to school together our whole lives."

"I know. I'm still trying to convince my mom to let me stay. She hasn't made up her mind one hundred percent. She's still thinking about it."

For the rest of the ride home, I just sit and listen to the music and to Dad's singing. He knows every lyric, even the ad-lib parts. I feel sadness burning in my chest, tears gathering in my eyes. But I hold it in, look out the window for license plates from other states. I don't call any out, I just keep count in my head.

When we pull up to KiKi's house, I say goodbye and whisper, "I really hope your mom lets you stay."

"Me too."

When we get home, Dad lies down for a short nap. Mom is already fixing dinner, and Rose is in her bouncer smiling and making noises, as usual. "All hands on deck, Ray," Mom calls out. Ray is sitting in the living room, entranced in his game.

He comes into the kitchen and Mom starts giving out responsibilities. While we help Mom get dinner ready, I tell her all about ice-skating and how it wasn't as scary as I thought it would be and that I want to go back and practice more so I can get as good as KiKi. "And speaking of KiKi..." I tell Mom that KiKi might not be returning to Vernon for middle school. "I don't want to be there without her," I say.

For the next fifteen minutes, Mom lists all the reasons why this might be a good thing and Ray tries to make me feel better by reminding me that KiKi won't be that far away, that we'll still get to see each other after school and on weekends. He is trying really hard to make me happy about this. "And middle school is fun, Ryan. You'll like it. You get your own locker and you don't have to stay in the same classroom the whole day."

Talking about sixth grade makes the sleeping butterflies in my belly wake up and start flapping around. I change the subject. "Mom, I, uh, I've been meaning to talk with you about something."

"Well, this sounds serious," Mom says. "What's wrong?"

"Nothing's wrong—"

"Something is definitely wrong," Ray says. "You have that I'm-in-trouble-and-I-know-it voice."

"Ray—let your sister talk."

"I didn't do anything to get in trouble. I wanted to talk about Grandma's birthday surprise."

"What about it?" Mom asks.

"She doesn't want it."

"Oh, Ryan, your grandmother always says she doesn't want to celebrate her birthday, but believe me, she'll love this."

"But what if she doesn't? And what if she gets mad at me because I've known all this time and haven't told her about it?"

"Ryan Hart, you better not utter one word about this party," Mom says. "It is a surprise."

"I know. That's the problem. Everyone is in on this big surprise that Grandma doesn't even know about and she's told me she doesn't want anything but rest."

Ray says, "She says she doesn't want it because she doesn't know it's happening. If she knew how many relatives and friends were coming from out of town, she'd be talking about it all day." Ray mocks Grandma's voice and says, "Aw, you all are too kind. You did all this for me? For me?" He laughs and switches back to his regular voice. "Trust us, she's going to be happy." Then he walks over to me and puts one arm around me, giving me a side-hug. "And you'll love middle school, even if KiKi isn't there. Everything is going to be fine."

Pranks

It's rained every day this week, but at least the days went by fast. It's already the weekend and I am having what Mom calls a lazy Saturday, taking my time getting up and dressed for the day. Mom and Rose are on a Mommies and Babies date at a local coffee shop and Dad is sleeping. He uses earplugs during the day so there's no way he'll hear anything I do. But that's just it. There's not much to do. Ray has the living room occupied with Aiden and Logan. They had a sleepover and kept me up all night long because they were playing video games and then started making beats and freestyling. I asked Ray to be quiet once and he told me, "You're not Mom, I don't have to listen to you," and so I went and got Mom, who told them the same thing, to be quiet so Rose could sleep. (But I needed quiet, too.) They must have stayed up super late, because the morning is almost over and they are still sleeping. Mom never lets us sleep in like this. Even on days when we have nothing to do, she still wants us to get up and get dressed. She is always bending the rules for Ray. I think it's because he's the oldest.

Here I am tiptoeing around during the daytime because they are too tired to get up. I can't watch TV because they are sprawled out in the living room. I think of a way to mess with them. This would be the perfect time to have cymbals that I could clash extra, extra loud. But who has cymbals lying around their house unless they're a musician? I think maybe I could put something up their noses. But that wouldn't work because I can only do one at a time and once I do Ray, he'd wake up screaming and then the prank would be ruined for Aiden and Logan. I think and think. If they were in Ray's room, I'd figure out a way to lock them in there. Let them spend all the time they want together. That's really what I want to do. Prove a point that they can't just stay up all night and then sleep all day while taking up all the space in the living room.

An idea comes to me.

Since they want to be together, I'll keep them together.

I tiptoe to the closet in the hallway where Mom keeps all her knitting supplies. There's yarn in the way back that she bought on sale but she ended up hating the color after all, so now it sits in the back of the closet collecting dust. I pull it out and start working on my master prank, tying them all together so when they wake up they can't move.

I have to move extra fast but extra careful all at once so that I don't wake them. I know Ray can sleep through anything, but I'm not sure about Aiden and Logan. I do them first just to be safe and get it over with. I make the knots tight enough so they'll have to struggle a bit to break free but not so tight that their wrists and ankles will hurt. Before any of them wake up, I finish. Three sleeping best friends connected as one. I laugh and go back into my room. I guess I'll read a book since I can't watch TV in the living room.

Maybe forty-five minutes pass, maybe a whole hour. I lose track of time because it's taking so long for them to wake up and then, just as I am turning the page in my book, I hear Ray screaming, "Ryan! Ryan!" and Aiden and Logan are yelling.

I run into the living room. "Oh, you're awake? Good afternoon."

"Ryan, stop playing. Untie us now."

"But don't you like being together? Don't you want to spend all your time together?"

"Mom?! Mom?! Ryan is—"

"Mom isn't here. And Dad is sleeping." I put my hand on my hip for extra attitude.

"This isn't funny. I have to use the bathroom," Aiden says.

And when Ray says, "Me too," I know I need to

speed this up a bit because I will get in serious trouble if any of them have an accident.

"Apologize," I say.

"For what?"

"For being rude and getting smart with me last night and for being in here all morning."

Logan says, "Sorry, Ryan."

"I'm not asking you to apologize. I'm talking to Ray."

I go into the closet and get Mom's fabric scissors. When I walk back over to the sofa, I stand in front them holding them up in my hands. "Apologize and I'll cut the yarn."

Ray wiggles and tries to figure out a way to get his wrists and feet free. "We don't need you to cut us free."

Aiden says, "Uh, I think we do. I really, really need to go."

I look at Ray. "Apologize."

"Ryan, I'm sorry for being rude to you last night."

"And?"

"And we should have slept in my room so that you could move around the house without having to worry about us."

"Apology accepted." I cut Aiden first because seriously, if he goes to the bathroom on this sofa my parents will put me on punishment for the rest of my life. He runs to the bathroom once he's loose, saying *thank you* over and over.

And then I cut Logan, since he was the one to apologize first. When I get to Ray he says, "I'm telling Mom."

I shrug my shoulders like I don't care but inside I wonder if Mom will be upset and if I'll get in trouble.

Ray gets up, rubs his wrists, and says, "Actually. I won't tell Mom. Or Dad. I'll take care of it myself. Come on, Aiden and Logan, let's go to my room."

"Wait, what does that even mean—you'll take care of it yourself?"

"Revenge, Ryan. When you least expect it."

FASHION & STYLE

WHEN MOM GETS BACK from her Mommies and Babies date, she drops me off at Grandma's so I can get my hair done. Grandma has her gospel playing extra loud today. I hear it as soon as I step on the porch. I ring the doorbell, not sure if she'll hear me with all the music going, but she answers the door with a big smile on her face.

Grandma gets started right away on my hair. "So you want to wear it out, huh?"

"Yes. A big Afro like in the photo on your dresser."

"I'll braid the front and it'll be like a headband of sorts. Help to keep your hair in place so it won't fall on your face." Grandma starts parting my hair. "Plus, it will be really cute." She styles the front of my hair in tiny braids. "Can't believe how fast time is passing. We're just about at the end of the year," she says. "Soon you'll be starting the second half of fifth grade."

Here it comes. All the adults in my life keep talking about me moving on from fifth grade and starting middle school, but it's not something I want to talk about. Not since KiKi told me she might go to another school. I don't want to do middle school without her. I'm already doing so much without Amanda.

"Grandma, when you first moved to Portland, did you miss your friends?"

"Oh, sure I did. I think I cried off and on the whole trip here. I'm a Southern girl who knew nothing about the Pacific Northwest. Your grandfather got a good job here, so it was the right thing to do. But I was leaving behind all my family and friends." Grandma is quiet for a moment and then I think she realizes why I asked her about missing her friends. And this is why I love Grandma so much. Instead of trying to make me feel better or telling me it's not a big deal because KiKi will still live close by and I can still walk to her house and see her at church and on weekends, she says, "I hope you and KiKi stay at the same school."

"I hope so, too."

Grandma fluffs my hair out, sprays it with her top secret hair care moisturizer, and twists some of my strands in her fingers, defining the curls. She gets her handheld mirror and shows me my new hairstyle.

"I love it!"

Now that Grandma is finished with my hair, I ask her the question I've been wanting to ask since I got here. "Grandma, can we look at more photos of you when you were younger?" Ever since I saw that photo of Grandma with her fro, I realized I don't know much about Grandma when she was my age or even a teenager for that matter.

"Well, sure," Grandma says. She takes a photo album off one of the bookshelves in the living room and we sit together and flip pages, turning back time and looking into her past. The book starts with Grandma as a baby. It is a black and white photo and it looks worn and fragile even behind the plastic sleeve. "Grandma, baby Rose looks just like you!" I say.

"She sure does. Isn't that something, how genes pass down and down?"

We keep looking through the book and I see photos of Grandma in her teen years, wearing the most stylish skirts and tops, her hair always perfect and in place. "You could have been a model," I tell her.

Grandma smiles.

For some reason I feel closer to Grandma just by seeing photos of her from before she was a grandmother. In these photos, she is not taking care of children or grandchildren, she is not running errands or donating her time and treasures, she is not offering advice and taking a head full of chaos and making something beautiful. In these photos, she is just a girl. Just a girl who doesn't know she will marry one day and have two daughters and that her grandchildren will love her more than the stars love to cling to the sky.

Grandma closes the book. "All right, I need to get you back home," she says. "I'll show you more one day. But you'll have to remind me. This old mind of mine forgets things sometimes."

"I won't let you forget," I tell her. This is a promise I'll make sure Grandma keeps.

16

ANTICIPATION

THE DAY BEFORE THANKSGIVING, guests start arriving for Grandma's birthday celebration. It's so hard to hide them all or not talk about them because when Grandma calls, she asks, "What are you doing?" and I can't tell her that I'm spending time with Ms. Holmes, her best friend from childhood.

"Just hanging out," I tell her.

"Oh, good. You and Ray spending some time together, huh?"

"Yeah." Technically, it's not a lie. Ray is here, too. We just aren't speaking to each other. I keep waiting for him to make his revenge move, so all week I've been checking my seat before I sit down and looking under my bed before I go to sleep. Nothing so far. But I know it's coming.

Grandma says, "Okay, well, put your mom on the phone. I want to know if she needs me to bring anything else for dinner."

"Oh, um, Mom isn't here. She's . . . she's out." The truth is Mom is at the train station picking up family who are coming from Seattle.

"Where's your sister?"

"With Aunt Rose."

"Have your mom give me a call when she gets a chance. Okay?"

We hang up the phone and I take a deep breath. I got through it without ruining the surprise.

While we wait for Mom to get back, Ms. Holmes tells us stories about Grandma. I love learning about what Grandma did and how she was when she was my age. Ms. Holmes is in the middle of telling us about the day Grandma moved to Portland. "I cried and cried. I just couldn't fathom being so far from my best friend. And listen, we weren't babies at the time. We were married by then—grown women—and still, I felt like nothing would be the same without her living just a few miles away." Ms. Holmes takes a sip of the tea I made her, then says, "But we wrote letters, called each other often, and we kept in touch. All these years, never once have we lost contact with each other."

The doorbell rings. I'm assuming it's Aunt Rose bringing baby Rose back in time for a nap. Mom should be back any minute. Ray gets up to answer the door. He looks through the peephole, then turns and whispers as loud as a whisper can sound, "Grandma's here! What are we going to do? Grandma's here!"

"On the porch? Right now?" I ask.

"She's here."

The doorbell rings again.

"Um, Ms. Holmes, I—we . . . we've got to hide you. Grandma can't know you're here."

"My Lord, she's always meddling. Mess around

and ruin her own party. Okay, where do you want me?" Ms. Holmes stands up, teacup in hand.

"Um, you can go in my room," I tell her. "Follow me." I bring her to my room because I know for sure that it is clean and that my desk is neat enough for her to set her tea down in between sips, with plenty of books for her to look through if she wants. "Please, please don't come out," I say.

"You have my word."

By the time I get back into the living room, Grandma is inside taking off her coat and explaining why she's here. "Thought I'd stop by," she says. "Ryan told me the two of you were hanging out. And I know you are older now and can stay home by yourselves, but I just wanted to come and check that everything was okay. I'll stay till your mom gets back. What are you up to? Watching a movie?" Grandma sits down on the sofa, makes herself comfortable.

Ray looks at me like he doesn't know what to do.

"Grandma, we're fine. Really. Mom will be back

soon. We don't want you to think you have to baby-sit us."

"Babysit? You two are my grandchildren. I never count it as babysitting when I'm spending time with you."

The thing about having an (old) new tiny house is that you can hear everything happening outside. I usually don't like this but today, it's a good thing because I can hear Mom's car pulling into the drive-way. "Be right back," I say. I run out the back door, try to open it quietly so Grandma doesn't hear it. I wave Mom down before she walks to the front of the house. And now I am loud-whispering like Ray was. "Don't go to the front door. Grandma's here. Grandma's here—in the house." I see two people with Mom who I don't know. Immediately I know they are family because they look just like Grandma. I motion for them to come to the back door.

Mom says, "You know, I thought that was her car but then I thought, it couldn't be. Is she in there with Ms. Holmes? Does she know everything?"

I explain the situation and then tell Mom my plan. "So, I think I should bring them in the back door and sneak them to my bedroom and you should go through the front like normal and distract Grandma."

Mom takes a deep breath. "Okay. Yes, good thinking. Let's, let's do that."

I sneak these relatives that I've never met inside. We'll do proper introductions later. They seem nice and not surprised at all that Grandma is about to mess up her whole birthday.

My plan works.

Grandma is busy talking about the blessings that have come this year, sounding like she's gearing up for the testimony service tomorrow.

Once Mom comes through the door, she stops her trips down memory lane. "Well, here you are."

"Mom, what . . . what a surprise to see you here." Mom hugs Grandma.

"I just came by to check on them while you were gone. You know I don't like them being in the house alone."

It's always awkward when Grandma fusses at Mom, but I guess even moms get fussed at by their mothers. Somehow, Mom gets Grandma to leave. As she's walking out the door, Aunt Rose is coming up the stairs carrying baby Rose.

It's a revolving door of family coming in and out, in and out today.

Grandma waves goodbye, says, "See y'all tomorrow. Love you."

That night, before I go to bed, I check and check to see what Ray is up to. He promised revenge so many days ago, but he hasn't done anything yet. There's nothing sticky on the doorknob of my bedroom, nothing hanging over the top of my door that'll fall on me when I walk under it, no tacks in chairs, no spooky noises at night.

Maybe he forgot. Or maybe he's plotting and planning. Maybe this is a part of the prank—making me wait. This is torture not knowing what he's up to or when he's going to strike.

How long is he going to keep me in suspense?

THANKSGIVING

THE DAY IS HERE. Thanksgiving and Grandma's birthday. It's a tradition for us to go to church on the morning of Thanksgiving. It's usually a short service—a few songs, time for people to share testimonies of the blessings God has given, and then a short sermon. Grandma is sitting next to Mr. Simmons. They spend so much time together now that when I see Grandma and don't see Mr. Simmons, it feels strange. During prayer, Mr. Simmons nudges me, reaches in his pocket, and gives me a Werther's Original. The best kind of hard candies. No wonder he and Grandma get along. These are her favorite, too.

He slides it to me and whispers, "A little Thanksgiving treat."

Is he really giving me permission to eat candy in church? He smiles, then whispers, "Hurry and put it in your mouth before everyone opens their eyes."

I laugh a little and do as he says.

After prayer, Deacon LeRoy says, "Testimony service is now open." He lifts his hands as an invitation to welcome anyone from the congregation to the podium at the front of the sanctuary. The first person who shares tells us how she is thankful for her health after such a hard year of sickness, and the next person says he is thankful for a promotion at work. Then, to my surprise, Mom stands, hands Rose to Grandma, and walks to the podium. As she makes her way, people clap and say *Amen* before she's even said anything.

When Mom gets to the front of the room, she takes a deep breath and looks out at us. I wonder if she is nervous, if she is realizing that standing up in front of a big congregation to speak is terrifying.

I get nervous for her even though I am safe in my seat and don't have to say a word. This happens sometimes—feeling anxious for other people when they have to do something important. Like KiKi when she sings a solo—even though I know she's going to be amazing. I always get butterflies when she sings, and midway through her song, the nervousness goes away and I feel nothing but pride. Maybe that will happen now while Mom is saying, "I'm usually not one to say a lot but I had to take a moment and share how thankful I am to just be here today. There's been a lot of change for my family lately and while so much of it has been hard, I stand here today so thankful that in these hard times God placed family and friends in my life to help me through it all. I am so thankful for my three children, who teach me something every day."

I smile when Mom says this and I wonder what lessons I've taught her. I have never thought about me teaching Mom something. Mom says more about Dad losing his job, and us having to move, and how much she loves having baby Rose but how little sleep she is getting. Then she says, "And not to mention all that is happening in our world. So much going on. But I tell you what, I now understand what the elders used to sing about when I was a child." Mom takes a deep breath and starts singing. Her alto voice fills the sanctuary.

This joy that I have,
the world didn't give it to me.
This joy that I have,
the world didn't give it to me.
This joy that I have,
the world didn't give it to me.
The world didn't give it
and the world can't take it away.

As Mom walks back to join us on the pew we are sitting on, the congregation starts singing the rest of the verses, exchanging new words for joy. First love, then peace. We all sing in unison.

This peace that I have
the world didn't give it to me.
This peace that I have
the world didn't give it to me.
This peace that I have
the world didn't give it to me.
The world didn't give it
and the world can't take it away.

SURPRISES

SINCE GRANDMA IS THE one who asked me to make her a cake for her birthday, I guess I'm not ruining the surprise by baking it while she's here, but still. I'd rather do it without the pressure of her being nearby. She decided to come over right after church instead of going home, just to come back out again for dinner. All the guests from out of town are either at their hotels getting ready or out sightseeing before coming over.

Ray comes into the kitchen, goes to the fridge, grabs the orange juice jug, and gulps the last bit that's left. He walks out of the kitchen not saying a word to me. His silent treatment continues and I just want to call a truce and end all of this.

But right now, I can't worry about Ray. I have to make the perfect cake for Grandma. I'm doing just what she asked for—a chocolate spice cake. But this time I am upping it a bit and making it five layers instead of two. Mom keeps coming in and asking if I need help and I tell her that I am fine, that I can do it all by myself. This is my gift to Grandma.

Once the batter is ready to go into the oven, I get all five rounds in and set the timer. Just as I am about to lick the beaters (and the bowl), Mom comes into the kitchen and catches me in the act. "Ryan, I really wish you wouldn't do that."

"But it's the best part."

"It's not good for you." She takes the beaters out of my hands and puts them in the sink. "You should go ahead and wash the dishes you aren't using any-more. Good cooks have to clean as they make."

After I wash the dishes, I go into the living room, where Grandma is holding Rose. The TV is on a channel that's playing *A Charlie Brown Thanksgiving*.

We watch and pass Rose around until Mom says it's time to put her down. No more holding her because she does not want Rose to get spoiled. I wonder if that's true, that babies become spoiled if you hold them a lot. Seems like they'd just feel loved and know that someone cares about them.

The timer dings and Grandma says, "Sure does smell good, Ryan." She smiles and tells me, "I guess I'll have to pace myself—can't eat too much for dinner so I can have some room for birthday dessert."

I go into the kitchen, pull the oven open as gently as I can and stick a toothpick in all the rounds. No cake comes out, which is the sign that the cake is ready, but the color doesn't look right. It looks much lighter than the last time I made this recipe.

Maybe I do need Mom to help me.

I call her into the kitchen. "It doesn't look right, but I think it's done."

I can tell by Mom's face that she doesn't like the look of the cake, either. "Hmm. Maybe just let it bake for five more minutes. But watch it."

I set the timer again, turn on the oven light, and sit

on the kitchen floor waiting and praying. I cannot mess up Grandma's cake. This is all she wanted and people are here out of town and this will be their first time having my cooking, and my cake is the only dessert. I cannot mess up this cake.

The timer dings.

I open the oven. Not much has changed, but I take the pans out anyway because I don't want the cake to be dry. I set them on the counter, put a towel over them, and let them cool. The whole time waiting and praying, waiting and praying.

The cakes cool and it's time to ice and stack them. Everything is working perfectly until I get to the fifth round. It won't come out of its pan. I hit the side, take a knife and try to shimmy it out until finally it starts to fall into my hand. And by fall, I mean half of it falls to the floor and the other half is stuck in the pan. "No!" I don't mean to alarm everyone.

Mom calls out, "Everything okay?"

I hesitate. "Y—y-y-yes." I'm not going to make a big deal about this. Just problem solve and figure it out myself. I throw what's on the floor in the trash, leave the rest in the pan for now, and decide that I'll make a four-layer cake instead.

Icing the cake is my favorite part. Ever since Dad taught me how to decorate cookies, I've been practicing my icing design skills and I have something extra special planned for Grandma. I work on it carefully, trying my best not to mess up any of the piping. And finally, it's done. I step back, look at the cake from all angles. Fix all the mistakes.

Ray walks in the kitchen again, going into the fridge like always. "Whoa," he says. "That looks amazing." He's broken his silence. Who would have thought those would be his first words to me? Maybe he's calling a truce, waving a white flag. "I've never seen you make something like this. What's it for?"

I whisper, "Grandma's birthday. It's dessert after tonight's dinner."

"That's for Grandma's surprise party?" Ray shouts.

"Ray!" I put my finger up to my mouth, telling him to be quiet. "Don't ruin the surprise."

"Wait, you just made that cake for everyone to eat...tonight?"

"Yes. Grandma asked me to—" I don't finish my sentence because the look on Ray's face is confusing me. He looks sick, scared. "What?" I ask. "Why are you looking at me like that?"

"Ryan, did you . . . did you put sugar in your cake batter?"

"Of course."

"From there?" Ray points to the sugar jar on the counter.

"Yes."

Ray backs up a little. "Okay, so, here's the thing... I didn't even know you were baking something for Grandma's party...I did this days ago and kept waiting for you make something. You always bake, but you haven't made anything in days. How was I supposed to know?"

"Know what? What are you talking about?"

"I, well, it's your fault, Ryan. I was getting you back. I promised revenge, so I was just playing a prank on you. I didn't know this was going to be a big-deal-happy-birthday-happy-Thanksgiving cake for Grandma."

"What did you do, Ray? What. Did. You. Do?"

"I switched the sugar and salt. You didn't use sugar in your batter today. That was salt."

I just stand there staring at Ray. My heart is pumping so fast, I have to take deep breaths to slow it down. And just when the tears are about to fall, I realize that this is the prank. Ray wants me to get upset and then he'll say something like *tricked you* or *gotcha*. I'm not falling for it. "I don't believe you. You knew I was making a cake for Grandma. You knew I was baking it today. You're just messing with me. The cake is fine. You've got to do better than this to get me, Ray."

"I promise you, I am telling you the truth. The prank was me switching the sugar for salt. And I promise you if I knew you were baking for Grandma's birthday, I wouldn't have done this." Ray's cheeks are red and he starts pacing.

I pick up the pan that has the damaged leftover

cake and break off a piece and eat it. I run to the trash can and spit it out as soon as I can. "Ray! Ray, you've ruined everything!"

Grandma comes into the kitchen. "Hey, hey, what's all this racket? Your mom is putting Rose to sleep and your father is resting."

"Ray ruined everything!"

"What do you mean? What's wrong?" Grandma asks.

I look at Ray because he really should be the one to tell her since he's the one who messed up her birthday gift. He doesn't say anything.

My chest is heaving up, down, up, down. And I know I am screaming, but I can't control my voice. It is loud and raging and flooding out of me. "Ray—my prank was not this bad. I didn't ruin anything for you. You took it too far! You ruined everything."

"Listen, now. Stop all this yelling and tell me what's going on." Grandma looks over at the cake. I see her eyes sparkle just a bit and that just makes it even worse.

I take a few deep breaths, calm myself down, and say, "Grandma . . . your cake. It's . . . it's all messed up. Ray switched the sugar with salt and I didn't know and now it tastes like salty dirt."

"But Grandma—the reason I did it is because—"

"Ray, hush." Grandma's eyes have lost their sparkle.

The three of us are silent, except for my heavy breathing and heavy tears.

Grandma, for the first time ever, looks like she doesn't know what to do or say. Finally, she takes my hand and says, "Sweetheart. It's just cake. And you know what—I probably didn't need it no way. You can make that cake again another time. I'll deal with Ray, but just know that nothing has been ruined."

"But that's not true. It is ruined. There will be no dessert tonight at your birthday party!"

"Ryan!" Now Ray is yelling.

"What party?" Grandma asks.

Now I am really a puddle of tears because not only has Ray ruined her cake, but now I've ruined her surprise. I confess everything to Grandma. Whisper it because I don't want to let Mom know I am telling all the things we've been up to.

"Well, I'll be," Grandma says. It takes her a moment to realize everything I just told her. "Charlotte is here?"

"Yes," I say. "But you're not supposed to know and now it's all just a mess."

Ray finally speaks, his voice timid. "I'm sorry, Grandma. I'm sorry, Ryan. I really didn't know the salt would be in the cake you were making for the birthday celebration."

Grandma says, "I promise we will talk about consequences later. I mean, the two of you with this back and forth of pranks needs to stop. But . . ." Grandma looks at her watch. "For now, looks like we have a party to get ready for. Now, what are we going to do about this dessert?"

Ray and I just stand in the middle of the kitchen looking at her.

"We gotta get moving if we're going to redo the

cake. As a matter of fact, why don't we do cupcakes instead?"

Ray and I don't move.

"Come on, let's get it together. We've got to get these cupcakes made." Grandma reaches for the flour. "Ray, you're going to learn how to bake today. Get the eggs out of the refrigerator."

"Yes, ma'am."

"Ryan, where's that recipe?" Grandma asks.

We gather all the ingredients we need and start mixing the batter for the cupcakes.

I show it to her and say, "You shouldn't be making your own birthday dessert."

"Oh, it's fine. This way I'll know how to make it on my own when I get a craving."

Ray never, ever cooks anything, so to see him breaking eggs, stirring, and pouring oil is a sight to see.

We make the batter and pour it into the cupcake tins. Grandma puts the trays in the oven and then turns and whispers, "Don't worry, your grandma is pretty good at keeping secrets. And if I hadn't become a beautician, I could've been an award-winning actress." She winks. "I will act surprised, I promise. And, well, truth is, I'm so full of joy about this, I won't even have to act too much."

"Full of joy? How can you be happy right now?" I ask.

"Now, I didn't say I was *happy*. I have to say I am very disappointed." She looks at Ray when she says this. "I understand siblings joking around and all, but this is not okay. And like I said, I will deal with Ray. So, no, I'm not happy right now. But joy, Ryan? Joy is something deep, deep down. Joy isn't always based on how you feel, but what you know. And sometimes joy is happening even when frustration and sadness is happening. So, that's why I said what I said. Today, I am reminded of how much this family loves me. And my heart is truly overjoyed."

19

HAPPY BIRTHDAY

THE TABLE IS FULL of so many delicious dishes: smoked turkey, stuffing, baked mac and cheese, candied yams, green beans—perfectly made by Mom, with a little crunch, not soggy and slimy.

The house is full of so many of my favorite people. Grandma, Mr. Simmons, Uncle David and Aunt Rose, my cousins, Ella and Micah, KiKi and her mom, of course Ray and baby Rose, and all the guests who've come to be here for Grandma's birthday. Grandma was right when she said she could have been an actress. The way she cries and hugs everyone and keeps saying, "I can't believe this, I can't believe this," almost makes me wonder if she really didn't believe me and Ray. But then she winks at me and I know she is protecting our secret. And I know she is also telling the truth because when she sees Charlotte, the way she looks at her is the way friends look at each other when they've loved each other and cried together and laughed together and shared secrets and dreams.

Grandma makes her rounds through the room, greeting every single person who's here. We eat dinner and just before dessert, a few people give toasts. The cupcakes are on the table and soon every single one is gone. Mom takes her last bite and says, "I thought you were making a five-layer cake."

"Change of plans," I say.

"Well, this is even better. Bite-sized and easy to eat."

Dad stands and calls out to everyone to get our attention. "All right, we're each going to share something we're thankful for about our beloved mother, mother-in-law, grandmother, and friend. I'll start."

Dad says how thankful he is that Grandma is so helpful with baby Rose and that she is such a loving grandmother to me and Ray. Mom talks next and as each person goes, Grandma smiles bigger and bigger. No acting at all, the joy she is feeling is real.

ME + AMANDA – KIKI

MY CUPCAKES WERE a hit and everyone is telling me what a good baker I am (no thanks to Ray). The adults gather in the living room to watch the football game.

KiKi and I go into my room. "I can't wait to get to Amanda's tomorrow for our own Thanksgiving celebration. Are you already packed?"

"Yep," KiKi says. "I packed this morning. My mom said she'll take us first thing in the morning." When KiKi says this, she makes a face like it hurts to talk. She rubs her throat and sinks into my beanbag chair.

"Are you okay?"

"Mm-hmm."

"You sure?"

"My throat kind of hurts," KiKi says. She rubs her throat, and I see her pause before she swallows. Then, she says, "I'm so hot. Are you hot?"

This isn't good.

KiKi looks at me and blurts her words out loud, like a confession. "I don't feel good, Ryan. I think ... I think I'm sick."

"*Sick* sick, or just kind of sick?" I ask. There are levels.

"I think I'm really close to *sick* sick. Like, if we had school tomorrow, I'd probably have to stay home kind of sick."

Just then, there's a knock at my door. It's KiKi's mom. "Sweetheart, it's time to go."

KiKi moves slow like she is walking in quicksand.

KiKi's mom must be psychic or something. Before KiKi even says anything about her throat, her mom takes a long look at her and says, "You sick?" She turns her hand backward and holds it up to KiKi's forehead. "You have a fever. You definitely have a fever."

And right then, KiKi's eyes swell with tears. "But Mom, I'm supposed to spend the weekend at Amanda's with Ryan. We're going in the morning, remember?"

"You can't go if you're not feeling well."

KiKi cries harder. "But we've been planning this for weeks."

"Well, Ryan isn't sick. She can still go be with Amanda. The three of you will have plenty of time to have more sleepovers."

KiKi looks at me like she is asking me not to go without her. Like me admitting that I feel good is somehow betraying her.

"Let's get you home so I can get you some medicine. You need to lie down and rest."

Nothing I've planned for Thanksgiving is going the way I thought it would.

As soon as I get to Amanda's, Zoe runs up to me and says, "Guess who's about to be six years old?"

I joke with her and say, "Melissa?"

"Nope."

"Hmm . . . your mom?"

"Of course not," she says. She is a storm of giggles. "One more guess," she says.

"Amanda?"

"Wrong again! It's *meeeee*! My birthday is next month." Zoe jumps up and down, grabbing my hands so I can join her.

"All right, all right, let Ryan get in the door all the way. Give her some breathing room," Mr. Keaton says. "She's so happy you're here. She's been talking about this all week, counting down the days until Amanda's friends are coming."

Amanda says, "Let's go in my room. I want to show you something." She pulls me into her room and shows me the manicure setup she put together. "I thought it would be fun to paint our nails tonight," she says. "Too bad KiKi is sick."

"Yeah. I was just thinking that. Maybe we can call her later."

"Definitely," Amanda says. "But first, ready for pizza?"

"So ready," I say.

We eat pizza in the kitchen at the island. The whole time Zoe keeps asking if she can eat with us, but Mrs. Keaton tells her no, that it's special time for me and Amanda and tells her to leave us alone. But once I start teaching Amanda my cookie recipe, we let Zoe help out. When the cookies are cooled and ready for decorating, I show Zoe some of the tips Dad showed me. "All I can do right now with Rose is hold her, rock her to sleep, and feed her. I can't wait till my baby sister is old enough for me to spend time with her like this," I say.

Amanda says, "Oh, you can wait. Trust me."

As soon as she says it, Zoe drops the bowl of sprinkles, and the floor looks like it's been painted with polka dots. "Oops!" Zoe says.

Amanda shakes her head, jumps off her stool, and gets a broom. "See what I mean?"

I laugh. I'm sure being a big sister has its not-so-good

moments, but I'm hoping there will be more really great moments. "At least you're in the middle of two sisters. I have Ray as an older brother, remember?"

Amanda laughs. "Fair," she says.

After we clean up the mess in the kitchen, we go into the living room with our delicious decorated cookies and watch a movie. Amanda is the best slumber party host ever—she has printed out movie bingo sheets, so now I have to pay attention as we're watching so I can cross off squares. There's no prize, but still, it's something fun to play.

Just when we finish the movie, I think about KiKi and wonder how she's feeling. I think about how if I had to stay home while Amanda and KiKi were together, I would never, ever get over it.

After we paint our nails, we FaceTime KiKi's mother's phone while we wait for our nails to dry. Her mom tells us KiKi can only talk for a few minutes. "Hello?" KiKi sounds worse than when I last saw her. She is in her pajamas and a scarf.

"We miss you!" Amanda shouts out.

"I miss you, too. What all have you done so far?"

We fill her in on everything. "I saved some cookies for you," I tell her. "I'll bring them over when I drop off your gift."

"I forgot all about our gift exchange. I'm messing up everything," KiKi says. "I have something for both of you."

Amanda blows on her right hand and shakes her fingers to dry the polish faster.

I scoot closer to the phone to make sure KiKi can see both of us. "We can do the gift exchange now," I say. "It won't be the same, but we can hold up what we got for each other, and I'll bring you my gift and Amanda's gift the next time I see you."

"Okay, hold on." KiKi walks over to her closet and grabs two gift bags. "Ready."

"You first," Amanda says, pointing to me.

I give Amanda her gift bag and she opens it. "Homemade popcorn!"

I explain to them both that I got them the same thing. "But different flavors," I say. "Amanda, yours is chocolate banana popcorn. It's clusters of popcorn and dried banana chips drizzled in chocolate."

Amanda starts eating her popcorn right away. "How did you even think of this combination? This is so good."

"I know your favorite flavors of things, so I just experimented to get them all in one bite," I tell her. "And KiKi, yours is my version of the salted vanilla—"

"Like the kind at Saturday Market? I've been craving that ever since we went!"

I'm relieved that they both like their gifts. "Oh, and as a keepsake, there's a little note about what I love about each of you tied to the popcorn tin."

They thank me and KiKi says, "All right, I'll go next. Just remember that we said homemade gifts only . . . don't judge my DIY skills." KiKi coughs and holds her throat like that cough brought on the worst pain. "Sorry about that. Okay, here we go." She holds up her gifts to the screen at the same time. Two framed photos of the three of us when we were in the first grade. "So, of course I didn't make the frames, but I decorated them myself with words that describe you and quotes about friendship. Hope it's not too corny."

"I love it!" Amanda and I say at the same time.

I ask, "Where did you find that picture?"

"My mom had it in a photo album. She was looking through it for something else, and we couldn't believe it when we saw it. She forgot that she had it. So, we made copies and now we'll each have one."

Amanda's mouth is wide open. "We look so little in that picture." Then she gets up, walks over to her dresser, and comes back to us with two small boxes in her hands. "My turn. I kind of had the same idea as KiKi as far as half making it myself, half buying something to get me started." She hands me my box and opens KiKi's, holding it up to the phone so she can see. "I made us each a friendship bracelet. They're wooden bracelets that were pretty easy to color on and design. Our names are all on them, too."

We both thank Amanda for the bracelets. KiKi says, "I can't wait to wear mine."

"KiKi, time to get off the phone!"

"I'm sure you heard that," KiKi says. "I gotta go."

"Glad we got to open presents together. Feel better," Amanda says.

"Thanks for calling. Have fun tonight."

We all say bye and Amanda ends the call.

I put my bracelet on. It fits just right, and since it has so many colors, it'll match just about everything I wear it with. I'm going to write about this in my journal when I go home. So many good things are happening, I might run out of room.

RESOLUTIONS

I **SPEND THE REST OF** the weekend with Amanda. We call KiKi a few more times and eat Thanksgiving leftovers for breakfast. Grandma picks me up Sunday afternoon to take me back home. As we drive home, we listen to the radio. Holiday songs are on rotation now and I always know which songs are Grandma's favorite because she turns the volume up just a bit, and sometimes she sings along. Like right now, she is singing with the Temptations as they croon about dreaming of a white Christmas.

When the song ends, Grandma turns the music down and says, "Another year has come and gone.

You thinking of your New Year's resolutions yet, Ryan?"

"Not really," I tell her. "I've never made a New Year's resolution. I just make wishes on my birthday. Grandma, do you make New Year's resolutions or birthday wishes?"

"Both," Grandma says. "I save my wishes for things out of my control, treat those more like prayers. But my resolutions? Those are goals. Those, I have to work for if they're going to happen."

Another good holiday song comes on. Grandma turns the radio back up. "Lots of singers have sung this song. But no one sings it like Donny Hathaway," Grandma says. She sings along and I look out the window, thinking about wishes, prayers, and resolutions. My wish, my prayer—because it's not in my control—is for me and KiKi to stay at Vernon together next school year. *Please, God, please.* And my resolution is to learn more about people like Thelma Johnson Streat. I'm going to check out biographies and historical fiction from the library so I can learn more about the people Mom and Dad always tell me paved the way for me to be here.

And even though Grandma would disapprove, my other resolution is to get Ray back. I know it all worked out and Grandma had a wonderful birthday celebration. The best part is that she told me and Ray that she isn't even going to tell our parents—she promised that this whole thing will be a secret between the three of us. And that makes it even better. Ray thinks it's all resolved.

He won't even see me coming.

ACKNOWLEDGMENTS

To the women who show up for me time and time again: My sisters, Cheryl, Trisa, and Dyan. Kori Johnson, Dana Brewington, Chanesa Hart, Jonena Lindsey, Kendolyn Walker, Ellice Lee, Olugbemisola Rhuday-Perkovich, Ellen Hagan, Jennifer Baker, Linda Sue Park, Namrata Tripathi, Lisa Green, Ladi'Sasha Jones, Rajeeyah Finnie-Myers, Tokumbo Bodunde, Nanya-Akuki Goodrich, Moriah Carlson, Catrina Ganey, DéLana Dameron, Julia Torres, Meg Medina, Sue Shapiro, Linda Christensen, Shalanda Sims, and Velynn Brown.

Thank you to my editor, Sarah Shumway, and the entire team at Bloomsbury, and to my agent, Rosemary Stimola.